D0287789

Unicorn Princesses

PRISM'S PAINT
BREEZE'S BLAST
MOON'S DANCE

The Unicorn Princesses series

Sunbeam's Shine

Flash's Dash

Bloom's Ball

Prism's Paint

Breeze's Blast

Moon's Dance

Firefly's Glow

Feather's Flight

Unicorn Princesses

PRISM'S PAINT
BREEZE'S BLAST
MOON'S DANCE

Emily Bliss

illustrated by Sydney Hanson

BLOOMSBURY

NEW YORK LONDON OXFORD NEW DELHI SYDNEY

BLOOMSBURY CHILDREN'S BOOKS
Bloomsbury Publishing Inc., part of Bloomsbury Publishing Plc
1385 Broadway, New York, NY 10018

BLOOMSBURY, BLOOMSBURY CHILDREN'S BOOKS, and the Diana logo
are trademarks of Bloomsbury Publishing Plc

Prism's Paint first published in the United States of America in December 2017
by Bloomsbury Children's Books
Breeze's Blast and *Moon's Dance* first published in the United States of America in April 2018
by Bloomsbury Children's Books
Bind-up published in the United States of America in September 2018
by Bloomsbury Children's Books

ISBN 978-1-5476-0234-6 (bind-up)

Library of Congress Catalog-in-Publishing Data
for each title is available upon request
Prism's Paint LCCN: 2017010911
Breeze's Blast LCCN: 2017020574
Moon's Dance LCCN: 2017020573

Book design by Jessie Gang
Typeset by Westchester Publishing Services
Printed and bound in the U.S.A. by Berryville Graphics Inc., Berryville, Virginia
2 4 6 8 10 9 7 5 3 1

For Phoenix and Lynx

Unicorn Princesses

PRISM'S PAINT

Chapter One

In the top tower of Spiral Palace, Ernest, a wizard-lizard, scratched his long nose. He straightened his pointy purple hat and his matching cape. He picked up his magic wand. And he gazed down at a gray slug staring up at him from the tabletop. She twittered her long antennae. "I've been dreaming of this moment for months," she said. "Thank you so much for helping me!"

Ernest grinned. "It's my pleasure," he said. "And besides, I've been looking for excuses to practice my color-changing spells." He cleared his throat. He lifted his wand above his head. And then he stopped. "Um," he said, blushing, "could you remind me one more time what color you want to be?"

The slug smiled. "Ever since I was a tiny girl slug, I've longed to be the color of green grass. I'm tired of looking like a storm cloud."

"I've got to admit, it is awfully nice being green," Ernest said, looking down at his scaly, green hands. "And I've got just the right spell." He raised his wand again. But then he paused and his cheeks turned an even deeper shade of pink. "Oh dear, I've already forgotten your name. Could you tell me, just one last time?"

The slug rolled her eyes. "Sally," she said. "Sally the Slug."

"Oh yes, of course. That's right," Ernest said. "Now I'm ready." He took a deep breath. And he waved his wand as he chanted, "Sluggadug Swiggadug Sludgerug Slass! Make the Valley as Clear as Glass."

Ernest stared at the slug and waited. But her head, tail, and antennae remained gray as ever. He furrowed his brow. "Now, why didn't that work?" he asked.

"First of all," the slug said, frowning, "My name is *S*ally, not *V*alley. And second of all, you said, 'Clear as glass,' not, 'Green as grass.' "

Ernest slapped his palm against his forehead and groaned, "Oh dear!"

Just then, thunder rumbled and six bolts of silver lightning tore across the sky. The wizard-lizard rushed to the window and looked outside to see shimmering ribbons of red, orange, yellow, green, blue, and purple rising out of a valley in the distance. Soon, the streams of color formed a rainbow.

More thunder boomed. The rainbow flashed and glittered. And then, with a final bolt of lightning, the rainbow soared high

into the sky, flipped three times, and plunged downward.

"Oh dear!" Ernest exclaimed as he raced over to his bookshelf. He pulled out several thick, dusty books, looked at their covers, and tossed them across the room. Finally, he found a tiny, red book entitled *Undoing Color Spells*. He scanned the table of contents and flipped to the last page. He read out loud, "To reverse a spell that has drained the color from any part of the Rainbow Realm, find the missing rainbow and use it to repaint the land and creatures."

Still clutching the book, Ernest rushed out of his room and down the stairs, shouting, "The missing rainbow! We need to find the missing rainbow!"

Sally sighed and shrugged. She blinked her slate-colored eyes and twittered her antennae. "I guess I'll just have to keep being gray for now," she said. And with that, she glided off Ernest's table, leaving a shiny trail in her wake.

Chapter Two

Cressida Jenkins followed her older brother, Corey, off the yellow school bus. As soon as his feet hit the ground, Corey raced toward their house. Cressida knew he was in a hurry to play soccer with his friends before he started his homework.

As the bus pulled away, Cressida waved to her friends, Daphne, Eleanor, Owen, and Gillian. They waved back through the bus window, and Gillian shouted, "See you tomorrow, Cressida!"

"See you tomorrow!" Cressida called back. The bus rolled down a hill and disappeared around a corner. Cressida closed her eyes and took a deep breath. She listened to the birds chirping, and smiled as she felt the bright afternoon sun on her head and shoulders. Then, with a grin on her face, she skipped toward her family's house carrying her backpack and four rolled-up pictures she had painted in art class that day. Each was a portrait of one of the unicorns she had met in the Rainbow Realm—a magical world ruled by seven princess unicorns. In one painting, yellow Princess Sunbeam danced among the purple cacti in the Glitter Canyon. In another, silver Princess Flash raced up the Thunder Peaks. A third painting showed green Princess Bloom eating roinkleberries in the Enchanted Garden. And in the fourth, which she had finished only a few seconds before art class ended, purple Princess Prism posed in front of Spiral Palace, the unicorns' home. She had wanted to paint the other three unicorns—orange Princess Firefly, black Princess Moon, and blue Princess Breeze—but she had run out of time.

"How creative! What a vivid imagination you have," Ms. Carter, her art teacher, had said as she looked at Cressida's paintings.

"Thank you," Cressida replied. She knew better than to tell Ms. Carter, or any other adult, about her trips to the Rainbow Realm. None of the adults she knew even believed in unicorns. They most certainly wouldn't believe Cressida could visit the Rainbow Realm at any time by pushing a special key into a tiny hole in the trunk of an oak tree in the woods behind her house.

Cressida skipped past her neighbors' houses, up her driveway, and along the walkway that led to her family's brick house. All the while, her silver unicorn sneakers' pink lights blinked and flashed. "I'm home!" she called out, as she opened the gray front door.

"Hi, honey!" her mother called from the

living room. Her mother worked from home, and Cressida could hear the sound of typing on the computer.

Cressida carried her backpack and her unicorn paintings into her bedroom and placed them on her bed. In just a few minutes, she planned to start her math homework—a page of long division problems she felt excited to solve. But first, she decided to hang up her paintings. She grabbed a small jar of thumbtacks from her desk. Next, standing on her tiptoes on her desk chair, she tacked each unicorn portrait to her bedroom wall. After she finished, she sat on her bed and thought about her unicorn friends.

Just as Cressida turned to pull her math

folder from her backpack, she heard a high, tinkling noise, like someone playing a triangle. Her heart skipped a beat. She leaped over to her bedside table and opened the drawer. Inside, she found the old-fashioned key the unicorn princesses had given her. Its crystal ball handle pulsed and glowed bright pink—it was the signal the unicorns used to invite her to the Rainbow Realm.

Cressida shoved the key into the pocket of her orange corduroy pants and straightened her yellow T-shirt, which had a glittery picture of a rainbow-striped cat on the front. Then she dashed out of her room, down the hall, and to the kitchen, where she grabbed an apple. "I'm going for a quick walk in the woods!" Cressida called out to her mother. Fortunately, time in the human world froze while Cressida was in the Rainbow Realm, meaning that even if she spent hours with the unicorns, her mother would think she had been gone only a few minutes.

"Have fun, sweetheart," her mother said amid a flurry of typing.

Cressida ran out the back door, through her backyard, and into the woods. As she hurried along the trail that led to the giant oak tree with the magic keyhole, she ate her apple and wondered what the princess unicorns were doing that afternoon. She couldn't wait to see her magical friends, and to tell them all about the pictures she had painted.

But just before she reached the oak tree, Cressida stopped short.

Standing by the tree's trunk stood a unicorn Cressida didn't recognize. The unicorn looked as though she were made of colorless glass. Around her neck hung a ribbon, also clear, with a pendant that looked like a large crystal. In her visits to the Rainbow Realm, Cressida had never met a clear unicorn. And the other unicorns hadn't mentioned another sister.

For a moment, Cressida watched the unicorn, who was frowning as she stared at her transparent hooves.

"Hello," Cressida said, smiling.

The unicorn looked up, startled. Then her eyes lit up with relief. "Cressida! I thought you'd never get here!" the unicorn exclaimed. "We've been calling you all day. I got tired of waiting and decided to come find you."

The unicorn's voice sounded familiar to Cressida, but she couldn't imagine how she might have forgotten meeting a clear unicorn. "Have we met before?" she asked, feeling a little rude.

For a second, the unicorn looked hurt and confused. And then she laughed. "Of course you don't recognize me! I'm clear!" she exclaimed. "It's me, Princess Prism."

"Prism!" Cressida said, rushing over and wrapping her arms around the unicorn's neck. She expected Prism to feel hard and cold, like glass, but instead Prism felt warm and soft. "What happened?"

"Well," Prism began, "Ernest was casting spells this morning, and he accidentally drained all the color from me and my domain, the Valley of Light. And my magic amethyst isn't working the right way."

Prism glanced down at the clear stone on her ribbon necklace. All the unicorn princesses had gemstones that gave them unique powers. Prism usually wore a purple amethyst on a green ribbon that allowed her to turn objects any of the colors of the rainbow.

"Watch what happens when I try to use my magic," Prism said. She pointed her horn at Cressida's silver sneakers. The glass-like stone shimmered, and glittery light shot from her horn. Immediately, the sneakers turned clear, so both she and Prism could see Cressida was wearing one orange sock and one pink sock.

Cressida wiggled her toes and giggled. "I guess I should have worn matching socks today," she said.

"If my magic were working, I could fix that for you," Prism said, smiling. But then her face fell. "The worst part about my magic being broken is I can't make art. I've had exactly thirteen ideas for pictures today since my magic broke, and I haven't been able to paint a single one. It's terrible! Every time I've tried to paint, I've accidentally turned something clear."

Cressida nodded sympathetically. Often, while she was riding in the car or sitting at her school desk, she had ideas for stories she wanted to write and pictures she wanted to draw. She didn't like having to wait until later to start her creative projects, either.

"The only way to reverse Ernest's spell is to find the Valley of Light's missing rainbow and use it to repaint my domain," Prism explained. "You're so good at finding things and solving problems that I thought you could help me. So, will you? Please!"

"Of course!" Cressida said.

"Fantastic!" Prism said, turning toward the giant oak tree. "By the way," she said, kneeling as Cressida climbed onto her back, "where were you all day? We've been calling you for hours!"

"School, of course," Cressida said, gripping Prism's clear mane.

"School?" Prism replied, sounding confused. "What on earth is that?"

Cressida smiled. "It's where human girls and boys go all day to learn things. Like math and science and reading and history."

"Huh," said Prism. "I've never heard of that." She used her hoof to riffle through a pile of leaves at the base of the oak tree. "Now, where did I leave my key? Aha, here it is." She used her mouth to pick up an old-fashioned silver key with a crystal ball handle—just like the one Cressida still had in her pocket. The unicorn pushed the key into a hole at the base of the tree. Suddenly, the woods began to spin, so that first they looked like a blur of brown and green before everything went pitch black. Then, Cressida felt as though they were falling through space, and she held on tightly to Prism's mane.

With a gentle *thud*, Cressida and Prism landed in the front hall of Spiral Palace. At first, the room looked like a dizzying swirl of white, silver, pink, and purple. But soon enough, the spinning room slowed to a stop. Cressida grinned to see Sunbeam, Flash, Bloom, Breeze, Moon, and Firefly all lounging on large pink and purple velvet couches.

Chapter Three

The unicorn princesses leaped over to Cressida and Prism. Their magic gemstones glittered in the light of the palace's chandeliers, and their hooves clattered against the shiny, marble floors.

"Cressida!" Sunbeam exclaimed, dancing in circles on her gold hooves. "My human girl is back!"

"I told you she'd come," Bloom said, winking at Cressida and smiling reassuringly at Prism.

"We're so glad you're here!" Flash said, rearing up.

"Now that Cressida's here, it'll be no time before you can paint more pictures," Breeze said. "Sunbeam and I will even come help you look for the missing rainbow."

Firefly and Moon smiled at Cressida and flicked their manes and tails.

"You wouldn't believe how impatient Prism was getting," Sunbeam said. "After we called for you to come this morning, she paced the front hall for two hours. Then she insisted on going to the human world to find you."

"Cressida said she was at a place called 'school' all day and that's why she couldn't come earlier," Prism said. "Have any of you ever heard of that?"

The other unicorns furrowed their brows and shook their heads.

"Apparently, it's where human girls and boys go to learn things," Prism said.

Cressida giggled. "School is pretty fun," she said. "In my art class today, I painted pictures of Sunbeam, Flash, Bloom, and Prism. Next week, I'm going to paint Breeze, Firefly, and Moon."

Prism's eyes widened. "You get to paint at school? And you painted a picture of me? I want to go to school!" Prism exclaimed.

"Maybe sometime you can come with

me," Cressida said, excited at the thought of bringing a unicorn with her to school. Only humans who believed in unicorns were able to see them, and she wondered if any of the students in her class would even know Prism was there. She was certain none of the teachers would have any idea.

"Anyway," Flash said, smiling and rolling her eyes at Prism, "thank you so much for coming, Cressida. I know Prism is eager to get her magical powers back so she can paint. She's been moping around the palace all day and accidentally turning our furniture clear."

Cressida noticed two clear armchairs

and a clear couch on the far side of the room. "I'm excited to help," she said.

"Well," said Prism, swishing her tail, "are you ready to go?"

"Absolutely!" Cressida said. Just as she was about to climb on Prism's back, she heard rapid footsteps in the hallway that led to the palace's front room.

"Wait! Wait! Oh dear! Oh dear!" a high voice called out. Cressida smiled. She would recognize that voice anywhere: it was Ernest, the wizard-lizard.

"Cressida!" Ernest exclaimed, rushing toward her and trying to catch his breath, "before you go search for the missing rainbow, I wanted to give you a present."

"Uh oh," Bloom whispered, "Ernest is about to try to do even more magic."

"I heard that!" Ernest said, but then he smiled. "You're right that magic hasn't been going that well for me today."

"Just today?" Flash teased.

"Well," Ernest said, "it's true that occasionally my spells don't work out."

"Only occasionally?" Sunbeam said, winking.

Ernest rolled his eyes and cleared his throat. "I'm sure I can do this spell perfectly. I've been practicing all day."

"We're just kidding with you, Ernest," Breeze said. "We appreciate all your hard work."

Ernest grinned and took a deep breath.

He pulled his silver wand out of his cape pocket, raised it, and chanted, "Paintily Smaintily Colorfully Foo! Make a Rainbow Hawk and a Quaint Thrush, Too!"

Wind swirled around Cressida, blowing her dark hair into her face. And then, on the marble floor in front of her sat two birds, both blinking and looking confused. One was a large hawk with feathers that were every color of the rainbow. The other

was a smaller bird Cressida didn't recognize, wearing an old-fashioned black top hat and a little black coat. He carried a wooden walking stick.

"Oh dear!" Ernest mumbled, scratching his forehead. "Not again!"

Cressida giggled. The hawk was the most beautiful and colorful bird she had ever seen, even prettier than a peacock. "What are you looking at?" the hawk said haughtily. "Haven't you ever seen a rainbow hawk?" Then, he spread his wings, flew up to the ceiling, and perched on a chandelier. Cressida smiled and shrugged.

She looked down at the smaller bird. "Who are you?" she asked.

"Pleased to make your acquaintance,"

the bird said, bowing and tipping his top hat. Cressida noticed he had a speckled chest. "I'm a quaint thrush."

"What does that mean?" Cressida asked.

"Well," the bird said. "Quaint means a combination of cute and old-fashioned. And a thrush is a songbird." With that, the bird chirped a song that sounded like the kind of music people listened to long before there were computers, televisions, or even radios.

"Well, it's wonderful to meet you, rainbow hawk and quaint thrush," Cressida said, glancing up at the chandelier and then down at the floor.

"Oh dear! Let me try again!" Ernest said. He took a deep breath, waved his wand, and chanted, "Paintily Smaintily Colorfully Foo! Off with the Hawk and the Thrush to the Zoo! Make a Rainbow Smock and a Paintbrush, Too!"

Another gust of wind swirled around Cressida, and the hawk and the thrush disappeared. When she looked down, Cressida was wearing an art smock with a huge rainbow across the front. In its pocket was a long, clear paintbrush with soft bristles. "Perfect!" Ernest exclaimed. "I told you I could do it!"

"Thank you," Cressida said, admiring the smock and touching the soft bristles on the paintbrush. She couldn't wait to use it. "Thank you, Ernest! This is absolutely perfect," she said. "And it was also pretty

fun to meet the rainbow hawk and the quaint thrush."

"Of course!" Ernest said. He pulled a watch on a long chain out of his cape pocket and groaned. "Oh dear! I was supposed to meet Ally—or was it Cally?—fifteen minutes ago to try again to turn her blue. Or was it purple? Oh dear!" He turned and sprinted off, calling out, "Good luck, Cressida!"

Prism and the other unicorns smiled affectionately as they watched Ernest disappear down the hall. Then Prism looked at Cressida, "Now that you have your smock and your paintbrush, are you ready to come with me to the Valley of Light?"

"Absolutely," Cressida said.

"And you'll come help look, too?" Prism asked, glancing at Breeze and Sunbeam.

"Of course!" Breeze said. "I promised Sunbeam I'd teach her how to fly a kite this afternoon, but after that we'll come right over."

"Thank you!" Prism said. Then she kneeled down, and Cressida climbed onto Prism's clear back.

"I can't wait to paint again!" Prism called out as she trotted toward the palace's front door. Cressida felt a jolt of nervousness: she thought she would be able to find the missing rainbow, but she wasn't completely sure. She took a deep breath. All she could do was her best, she reminded herself.

Chapter Four

Outside Spiral Palace, Prism trotted along the clear stone path that led from the castle into the surrounding forest. For a moment, as she held onto Prism's mane, Cressida turned her head back toward the sparkling, white palace, shaped like a unicorn horn. It looked beautiful in the bright afternoon sun.

"I'm excited to see the Valley of Light," Cressida said, facing forward again.

"I can't wait to show it to you," Prism said, turning onto a narrow path that cut through a cluster of pine trees. "Even though it looks awfully strange right now."

Just then, they passed a meadow full of dandelions and buttercups. Prism slowed down. And then she stopped. "You mentioned you painted pictures of my sisters and me in . . ." Prism's voice trailed off. "What did you call it? Art snass?"

Cressida giggled. "Art class," she said.

"Does that mean," Prism asked, sounding excited, "that you like to paint?"

"I love painting!" Cressida said. "And I also like making things out of clay."

"Me too!" Prism said. "Well, I love painting! Clay is pretty tough to work with if you have hooves. Everything I try to make just turns out as flat as a pancake."

Cressida giggled.

"Anyway," Prism continued, "even though I'm desperate to fix my magic powers so I can paint again, there's something I've always wanted to do. And given that I'm clear at the moment, and that you love to paint, there won't ever be a better time. Are you ready for a little art adventure before we find the missing rainbow?"

"Absolutely!" Cressida said.

"Fantastic," Prism said, kneeling down. "It might be better if you walked, since getting to the village is a little tricky."

"The village?" Cressida asked, sliding off the unicorn's back.

Prism smiled mysteriously. "Follow me!" she said, and she flicked her mane and turned off the path and into the sea of yellow flowers.

As Cressida walked alongside Prism, she picked dandelions and wove together

two wreaths. She placed one on Prism's head and the other on her own.

"Thank you!" Prism said. "I've also always wanted to make a dandelion crown, but that's another thing that's impossible to do with hooves."

Cressida and Prism came to the edge of the meadow. "This way!" Prism said, taking a sharp turn down a steep hill dotted with thorny bushes. Cressida followed her, holding her arms out to her sides for balance as she hiked. Soon, they came to an even steeper hill, covered in shiny, green moss. "There's only one way to go down!" Prism declared as she sat on her hind legs, scooted to the edge of the hill, and glided down it. "Wheeeee!" she called out before she landed in a bed of pine needles at the bottom.

A slick, mossy hill seemed like the best slide Cressida could imagine. She sat down at the top of the hill and pushed herself forward. "Wheeeee!" she yelled, going much faster than she had ever gone on any playground slide. When she landed in the pine needles at the bottom, Cressida looked in front of her and sucked in her breath. Before them was a clearing filled with miniature houses made of moss, bark, twigs, leaves, and stones. Each house was painted in the most vibrant colors Cressida could imagine: magenta, robin's egg blue, lime green, fuchsia, teal, violet, and scarlet.

"Who lives here?" Cressida asked,

suddenly wishing her parents would paint their brick house—or even just their gray front door—one of the colors she saw here.

"You'll see," Prism whispered. "Do you like the colors of the houses? I used my magic to paint them myself!"

"I love them," Cressida replied.

Prism grinned and called out, "It's Princess Prism! Is anyone home?"

Cressida heard rustling noises. Soon, the houses' front doors opened, and out stepped creatures that looked like tiny girls with wings. They were, Cressida realized as her heart skipped a beat, fairies.

The fairies were even more colorful than their houses. One with turquoise skin, pink hair, and magenta wings straightened her orange dress. Another, with green skin, purple hair, and a white dress beat her red wings as she did a somersault in the air. More and more fairies, all with different colors of skin, hair, dresses, and wings stepped outside. Several jumped up into the air and hovered, beating their wings.

Just then, a fairy with dark blue skin, clover-colored hair, a lavender dress, and gold wings fluttered over to Cressida and Prism. As she got closer, Cressida noticed she wore a wreath made of daisies, violets, and roses. "Princess Prism!" the fairy called out. "I heard all about what happened with Ernest! I must say, you do look lovely even when you're completely clear. And what a beautiful dandelion crown you have."

"Well, thank you," Prism said, laughing. "Cressida, this is Titania, Queen of the Painted Fairies. And Titania, this is Cressida, our favorite human girl who has come to help find the missing rainbow."

"Hello, Cressida," Titania said.

"It's a pleasure to meet you," Cressida replied.

The fairy fluttered her wings. "I sure hope you can find the rainbow! Do you need help looking?"

"Thank you," said Prism. "I think we're in good hands with Cressida. Right now, I'm wondering if we could use some of your paint. We want to have a little fun before we start searching." Prism winked at Titania.

"I bet I know exactly what you want to do!" Titania said. "Luckily, my paint is already out and ready to use, since I was just painting my hair. It was lavender before, and I just changed it this afternoon. What do you think?" She twirled around so they could admire her long green curls. "I get bored if I don't paint it a new color at least twice a week."

"I love it!" Prism said.

"Me too," Cressida added, nodding.

Titania turned back toward them. "I'll go get the paint. And then the other fairies and I are going to start building a palace for ourselves out of pebbles." She looked at Prism. "When we finish, we're hoping you'll come paint it for us, provided you have your magic back."

"Of course!" Prism said.

Titania turned and flew inside a scarlet house with a bright pink roof and an orange door. A few seconds later she reappeared with a tray of metal cups, each filled with a different color of paint. "The paint is magic," Titania explained, handing the tray to Cressida. "It dries instantly. And instead of dipping your brush in water to clean it off, just tap it twice."

"Thank you so very much," Cressida and Prism said.

"My pleasure," Titania said. "Now I

need to go help the other fairies stack pebbles. When we're finished with our palace, it will look like a giant wing." Just before Titania turned and fluttered away, she said, "And please do let us know if we can help you later."

Chapter Five

Prism looked at Cressida and smiled nervously. "My sisters make fun of me when I say this, but I get tired of *always* being purple. And since I'm clear today, I was thinking that maybe you could, well—" Prism, embarrassed, looked down at her hooves.

"Do you want me to paint you?" Cressida

asked, so excited she couldn't help but jump up and down.

"Well," Prism said, "um, yes, if you wouldn't mind."

"I'd love to!" Cressida said. She looked down at her rainbow smock and pulled the paintbrush from the front pocket. As soon as she wrapped her hand around it, it hummed and glowed. She felt as though she were holding a magic wand. "What color would you like me to start with?" she asked.

"I have to admit, I've always wanted a pink stripe on my nose," Prism said.

Cressida gently lifted the dandelion crown from Prism's head and laid it on a nearby rock. She dipped the brush's bristles into a cup of bright pink paint, and the brush made a flutelike sound. Cressida smiled and painted a pink stripe from Prism's horn down to her nose.

"That tickles!" Prism said, twitching her nose at the feeling of the bristles. "How does it look?"

"Fantastic!" Cressida said. She tapped the brush twice with her other hand, and immediately, the pink paint disappeared from the bristles. "What color should I use next?"

"You decide," Prism said. "After all, you're the artist."

Cressida looked at the paints for several seconds, and then dipped the brush into a cup of fluorescent green paint. This time, the brush made a sound like a trumpet flourish. Cressida painted one side of Prism's head, including her ear, green. Next, she tapped the brush twice, dipped it into a cup of violet paint, and listened as it clanged like a bell. She painted the other side of Prism's head violet. Soon, Cressida had painted Prism's front legs orange, her hind legs ruby red, her back teal, her belly magenta, all four hooves canary yellow, and her mane and tail black.

"How do I look?" Prism asked, grinning and swishing her tail.

"Wonderfully colorful," Cressida said. "But you need some finishing touches!" She painted the ribbon around Prism's neck maroon and the glass-like amethyst mint

green. With peacock-blue and emerald-green paint, she decorated Prism's body with stars and hearts. And finally, she painted rainbow stripes all the way up Prism's horn. "All done!" Cressida said, beaming proudly as she looked at Prism.

"I can't wait to see it," Prism said, and she galloped to a nearby puddle. As soon as she leaned forward and saw her reflection, she whinnied with delight. "Oh, I love it! Cressida, I wish you could paint me different colors every day! This is so much more fun than just being purple all the time. Thank you!"

"That was the most fun painting I've ever had," Cressida said.

"Wow! What an amazing paint job," a

voice called out from behind Cressida and Prism. Cressida turned and saw Titania fluttering in the air. "Cressida, we'll have to invite you back to the Rainbow Realm to paint our palace once we finish building it!"

"I thought you said I could do that," Prism said, looking jealous of the attention Cressida was getting for her artwork.

Titania smiled reassuringly at Prism. "The palace will be big enough that you can both help paint it," she said.

Prism sighed with relief. "Thank you so much for letting us use your paint," the unicorn said. "And now, I think Cressida and I better go find the missing rainbow."

"See you soon!" Titania said. Before she fluttered away, she picked up Prism's dandelion wreath and put it back on the unicorn's head. "I wouldn't want you to forget your crown. You are a princess, after all," the fairy said.

"Thank you," Prism said. Then, she kneeled down and said, "Climb aboard! I know a short cut to the Valley of Light from here."

Swinging her leg over Prism's back and grabbing onto the unicorn's newly black mane, Cressida said, "Let's go find the rainbow!"

Prism galloped downhill for several minutes, weaving through patches of gigantic ferns and groves of pine trees. Then she stopped and said, "We're almost to the Valley of Light. Close your eyes!"

Cressida shut her eyes as tightly as she could. She felt Prism turn and then take several steps forward.

"Okay!" Prism called out. "You can look now!"

Chapter Six

Cressida opened her eyes and blinked in astonishment. Before her lay a valley in which everything was colorless and see-through. Diamond-like daffodils and tulips poked up from grass that looked like icicles. A gurgling river rushed and swirled down a bed of rocks that looked like giant crystals, as clear fish jumped in and out of the

rapids. Over the river arched a bridge that looked like it was made of ice. Nearby, trees with glass-like branches and clear leaves swayed in the breeze. Squirrels, chipmunks, and rabbits, all of which looked like glass animal figurines, played by the riverbank and chased each other through the grass.

"Wow!" Cressida said, inhaling. "It's beautiful!"

"It's much prettier in full color," Prism said. And then, to Cressida's surprise, tears formed in Prism's eyes. "What if we can't find the missing rainbow, and I can never make art again?" she asked.

Cressida wrapped her arms around Prism's neck. "I promise to do my best to find the missing rainbow. When I'm worried about a problem, I always feel better when I get started finding a solution. So, why don't we go ahead and start searching?"

Prism sniffled as tears streamed down her face, smearing the fluorescent-green and violet paint on her cheeks. She took a deep breath and nodded.

"How about if you look over there?" Cressida said, pointing to the grass and trees on the other side of the river. "And I'll look over here." She pointed to a cluster of gnarled trees behind them. "And pretty soon, Sunbeam and Breeze will be here to help us."

"I'm still so worried we'll never find it,"

Prism said, her voice shaking a little. "But you're right. The best thing to do is get started looking." She took one more deep breath, blinked the tears from her eyes, and trotted toward the bridge.

Cressida walked toward the trees. She decided to start by climbing one of them and looking out over the valley to see if she could spot the rainbow. She chose the tallest tree, grabbed one of the branches, and began to hoist herself up.

"Who's there?" a low voice rumbled.

Surprised, Cressida let go of the tree branch and jumped back down to the ground. And that's when she saw that the tree's trunk held two large eyes, a nose that looked like a misshapen lump of clay, two ears that resembled pieces of cauliflower, and a mouth. The tree squinted at her and said, "Are you a Rainbow Cat? If you are, you most certainly can't climb me!"

Cressida giggled. "My name is Cressida Jenkins. I'm a human girl," she said. "I'm friends with Princess Prism, and I'm here to help find the missing rainbow."

The tree squinted at Cressida and slowly leaned toward her, so his trunk creaked and groaned. "I've always wanted to meet a human girl, and the truth is I can barely see you at all. You don't see my glasses, do you? When all the color disappeared, it was so windy my glasses blew off my face. Usually, I'd ask the Rainbow Cats to get them. But not after the fight we had this morning. I'm never speaking to those silly cats again."

Cressida scanned the ground and spotted a large pair of clear glasses on a bed of

see-through moss. She picked them up and slid them over the tree's eyes.

"You are a human girl!" he called out, laughing. "I'm Trevor, by the way. Trevor the Tree."

Cressida giggled again. "It's a pleasure to meet you, Trevor. You don't know, by any chance, where the missing rainbow might be, do you?" she asked.

"It's the strangest thing," Trevor said. "We trees saw it fly straight up into the air, right in front of us, not six feet away. But none of us saw where it landed. And believe me, we were looking."

"I was sure it would land in my branches, and I was all ready to catch it," the tree next to Trevor added. "But I haven't seen a glimmer of it. I'm Trina, by the way. And this is my son, Tristan." With one of her branches, Trina pointed to a shorter tree who looked much less gnarled.

"It's a pleasure to meet all three of you," Cressida said. Then she looked back at Trevor. "Would you mind if I climbed you?" she asked.

"Be my guest," he said.

As Cressida hoisted herself up from one branch to another, she couldn't help but ask, "Who are the Rainbow Cats?"

"The Rainbow Cats used to be our best friends," Trevor explained, sounding angry. "They scratched our trunks, which was wonderful because we trees get itchy, and there are lots of places we can't reach with our branches. In return, we let them perch and sleep on our branches."

Trina scoffed and sighed. "That was before this morning," she said, "when those silly cats had the nerve to claim that their paintings are more creative than ours. They kept meowing that ours are 'boring.'"

"Can you believe it?" Tristan interrupted. "Those Rainbow Cats are terrible painters. They don't have thumbs, so they can't even hold paintbrushes! All they do is smear paint and make paw prints!"

"Exactly!" Trevor agreed. "That's what I told them! And then I explained our paintings are better because not only do we have thumbs and fingers, but we each have several hands. I can hold fifteen paint-brushes at once! Trina can hold seventeen. Tristan can only hold eight, but he hasn't grown all his branches yet."

"I see," Cressida said, pulling herself up onto Trevor's highest branch. She wanted to be careful not to take sides. The argument between the cats and the trees sounded like fights she had with Corey about who was better at bike riding or soccer. They were arguments that neither she nor Corey ever won, but they put both of them in a bad mood.

Cressida squinted as she scanned the Valley of Light for even the slightest glimmer of color. But everything—every tree, every blade of grass, every flower, every turtle, every squirrel, every chipmunk, and every rock—looked clear and colorless. Where, she wondered, could the missing rainbow be? It seemed like it should be easy to spot. Worry that she might not be able to find the rainbow—and that Prism would be absolutely miserable without her ability to make art—swelled within Cressida. She took a deep breath. "It has to be somewhere," she whispered to herself. "I'll just have to keep looking."

Cressida quickly climbed back down Trevor. "It was wonderful to meet you," Cressida said to Trevor, Trina, and Tristan. "And if you'll excuse me, I'm going to keep looking for the missing rainbow."

"Good luck!" the trees called out.

Chapter Seven

Cressida walked beyond the trees and through a field of clear wild-flowers, scanning the ground for the rainbow and trying to imagine where else she could possibly look.

As Cressida carefully stepped over a clear turtle sunning herself on a see-through log, she heard a loud meow, followed by purring. She turned to her right and saw, slinking toward her, two large, see-through cats. Cressida grinned with excitement. After unicorns, cats were Cressida's favorite animal.

Cressida decided the cats were about the size of the leopards she had seen on a recent trip to the zoo on a school field trip. "Hello," one of the cats purred, flicking her tail. "You must be Cressida. I'm Riley. And this," Riley said, nodding to the other cat, "is my best friend, Roxy."

"Prism told us all about you," Roxy said, purring and rubbing her head against Cressida's shoulder. Cressida giggled as Roxy's long whiskers tickled her neck.

"Poor Prism is absolutely miserable," Riley added, pushing her head against Cressida's hand. Cressida scratched Riley between her ears, and the cat closed her eyes and purred loudly. Then Roxy flopped down and rolled onto her back. Keeping one hand on Riley's head, Cressida kneeled and rubbed Roxy's belly with her other hand. Roxy purred and extended her legs straight up into the air.

Though Cressida thought she could spend hours petting the two giant cats, she also knew she had better keep looking for the missing rainbow for Prism's sake. "I'm wondering," Cressida said, "if either of you know where the missing rainbow is."

"We both saw it go up into the air, right

in front of those awful trees," Roxy said. She curled her lips into a snarl and flicked her tail when she said the word "trees."

"But we didn't see it land," the two cats said in unison.

"We haven't seen it anywhere," Riley said. "And we've been walking around the Valley of Light all day looking for it."

"We even skipped two of our catnaps to search for it," Roxy added, yawning.

Cressida felt a pang of anxiety. But then she took a deep breath. There must, she thought, be somewhere she wasn't thinking to look. As she continued to scratch and pet the cats, she turned toward Trevor, Trina, and Tristan. She imagined the rainbow sailing straight up into the air in front of them. Then she looked up toward the sky to see if there was anywhere it might have landed on its way back down. But all she saw above the trees was a brilliant, cloudless, blue sky.

Deep in thought, Cressida stared into the distance. Her eyes caught sight of a gray rain cloud hanging low in the sky. For a moment, she watched it. And then she jumped up and down. "I have an idea!" she exclaimed, eyes wide with excitement. "I need to find Prism right away!"

"We'll take you to her," Riley said, stretching and crouching down. "Climb onto my back."

Cressida's heart raced. She was going to ride a giant cat! She grinned as she slid onto Riley's back and wrapped her arms around the cat's soft, furry neck.

"Off we go!" Riley purred, and then she and Roxy sprinted through the grass, leaped right over the river, and bounded over several large rocks. Cressida held on tight, her face pressed against Riley's fur, as the cat soared through the air.

"I had no idea you could jump so high," Cressida said.

"It's our specialty," Riley purred.

Soon, Cressida, Riley, and Roxy found Prism behind a large, clear bush talking to Breeze and Sunbeam. Tears rolled down Prism's cheeks, which were now completely clear. Her dandelion wreath lay in a withered ball by her hooves. "We'll never find it," she wailed. "I'll never be able to paint again."

"Oh Prism," Sunbeam said, "I promise we won't stop looking until we find it."

"But can you think of anywhere else to look?" Prism asked.

Sunbeam and Breeze shared a nervous glance. "Honestly," Breeze said, "I can't."

Prism cried harder. Sunbeam glared at

Breeze and whispered, "Stop being so honest!"

Breeze shrugged.

"I'm sorry to interrupt," Cressida said, "but I have one last idea. I'm not sure if it will work, but I think we should try it."

"I'll try anything!" Prism sniffled.

"The first thing we need to do," Cressida said, "is hurry over to the trees before that gray cloud in the distance stops raining." She pointed to the cloud.

Prism smiled even though tears still streamed down her face. "Your idea isn't from something you learned at that place you call school, is it?"

Cressida giggled. "As a matter of fact, it is," she said.

Prism kneeled so Cressida could climb onto her back. "Let's go!" Prism said, and with that, the three unicorns and the two cats sprinted toward the trees.

Chapter Eight

Cressida, Prism, Sunbeam, and Breeze stood just in front of Trevor, Trina, and Tristan. Riley and Roxy hung back and began to wash themselves, unwilling to make eye contact with the trees.

Cressida looked at Trevor. "You said the rainbow flew straight up from here, right?" she asked.

"Correct," Trevor said, nodding so his trunk creaked.

Cressida pointed to the rain cloud she had spotted in the distance and turned to Breeze. "Could you create a gust of wind that will bring that gray cloud right above us?"

Breeze frowned. "But then it will rain on us," she said.

"It's true we'll get a little wet," Cressida said. "But we'll dry off. And this might be our best chance to find the rainbow."

"Well, okay," said Breeze, sounding doubtful. She pointed her shiny blue horn at the rain cloud. The aquamarine on her ribbon necklace shimmered before a beam of light blue, glittery light shot from her horn. Suddenly, a comet-shaped gust of blue wind swirled upward and bolted toward the rain cloud. In a few seconds the rain cloud shot back toward them, the blue gust of wind pushing it forward.

For several seconds, the cloud hovered just over their heads, drizzling on Cressida and the three unicorns. Prism frowned as all the paint ran off her body and pooled in puddles around her hooves, leaving her clear once again. Sunbeam flattened her ears backward and said, “I hate getting wet.” Breeze sighed and swished her tail impatiently. Cressida actually liked the feeling of the rain on her face and hair—it felt cool and refreshing.

When the rain lessened to just an

occasional drop, Cressida looked at Sunbeam. "Can you make the sun shine on us, as brightly as possible?"

"Gladly," said Sunbeam, flicking stringy, wet clumps of her yellow mane from her eyes. She pointed her horn toward the sun. The yellow sapphire on her chest glittered. A golden beam of glittery light shot from her horn. And then warm, bright sunlight shone down on Prism, Sunbeam, Breeze, and Cressida.

As the sunlight hit the thick, humid air, a rainbow appeared, dangling from the cloud. "There it is!" Cressida said, jumping up and down. "Now we need to get it before it disappears again!"

"Why would it disappear?" Prism asked,

looking confused. "Is this another thing you know about from school?"

Cressida giggled. "Yes! We had a science lesson in school where we learned that rainbows appear when the sun shines right after it rains. The reason is that even though we can't feel them, there are still raindrops hanging in the air, and each raindrop is like a prism. When the sun shines through the drops, a rainbow forms. The rainbow goes away when there aren't enough raindrops in the air anymore."

Sunbeam, Breeze, and Prism looked fascinated. "I always wondered where my name came from!" Prism exclaimed. "The more I hear about school, the more I want to go. Not only do you get to paint, but you also get to learn about prisms and rainbows." Then Prism's face fell. "How are we going to get the rainbow? Even if you climb to the top of Trevor, you won't be able to reach it."

"I have an idea," Cressida said. "But the Rainbow Cats and the trees will have to work together."

"No way!" Trevor said.

"Absolutely not," Trina added.

Tristan crossed two branches across his trunk and grimaced.

Cressida took a deep breath. "I know you're angry at the Rainbow Cats," she said. "But I wonder if you might try talking through your differences. Otherwise, Prism won't get her magic back. And you won't have your best friends to scratch your trunks."

Trevor, Trina, and Tristan glowered at the cats. But Trevor said, "You know, I admit my trunk has been awfully itchy today without the cats to scratch it."

Trina sighed. "My trunk is itchy, too," she said.

"Mine too," Tristan said, nodding.

Trevor looked down at his gnarled roots. "Well, I guess I'm willing to talk to the Rainbow Cats," he said.

Trina and Tristan nodded in agreement.

Cressida glanced at Riley and Roxy, who had stretched out in a particularly sunny patch of clear grass. Though they were pretending not to listen, Cressida could tell from their faces that they were paying attention.

"Well," Cressida said, feeling a little nervous, "I know you had an argument about whose artwork is better. And I bet you all feel hurt and angry. It makes sense to me that you'd also feel proud of your artwork, and the different ways you paint."

Riley and Roxy began to wash their faces. The trees frowned. "I think," Cressida said, "that the world would be an awfully boring place if everyone painted the same way. I'm glad there are many different styles and ways to paint. It's part of what makes looking at art, and making art, interesting. It's great that the trees paint by holding lots of different paintbrushes at once. And it's just as great that the cats use their paws to smear paint. Instead of arguing over whose artwork is better, maybe we could agree that your artwork is just different. And that those differences are wonderful."

The Rainbow Cats and the trees were silent. But Cressida noticed that the cats had stopped cleaning themselves. And the trees had thoughtful expressions on their faces. Finally, Trevor said, "I admit, it would be terribly boring if the only paintings in the Valley of Light were made by us trees." Trina and Tristan nodded.

Tristan looked at Riley and Roxy and said, "I thought those paintings you made last week with all the mice running on the rainbows were really neat. I never would have thought to paint that."

"Thank you," said Riley and Roxy.

"And we really liked those paintings you three trees made of your roots growing into the ground," Roxy added. "I never would have been able to come up with that idea."

"Thank you," the trees said in unison.

The Rainbow Cats and the trees looked at each other, but no one spoke. "Is there anything else you want to say to each other?" Cressida asked. "Sometimes, when I've had an argument with my brother or a friend, it helps us feel better if we say we're sorry. I always hate how I feel right before I apologize. But then I feel much better afterward."

Trina bit her lip. And then she said, "I'm sorry I said the trees are better at painting than the Rainbow Cats. I don't really believe that. I miss you, and I want to be friends again."

"Apology accepted," Riley said. "And I'm sorry I said the cats' paintings are better than the trees'. I only said that because I felt angry. I want to be friends again, too."

"I'm sorry, too," Trevor, Tristan, and Roxy all said at once. Then, they all laughed.

"Friends again?" Roxy asked.

"Most definitely friends again," Tristan responded. "And I'm wondering if one of you could scratch that place on my—" But before he could even finish his sentence, Roxy was sharpening her large, clear claws on the back of Tristan's trunk. He closed his eyes and grinned.

Cressida, Prism, Sunbeam, and Breeze exchanged looks of relief. "Good work, Cressida," Prism said.

Chapter Nine

Cressida looked up at the rainbow dangling from the gray cloud. She hoped she could get to it before it faded away. "Riley, could I ride you up to the top of Trevor? Then, if you jump as high and far as you can, I'll reach up and grab the rainbow."

"Absolutely!" Riley said. She crouched down, and Cressida swung her leg over the cat's back. "Up we go," Riley said, gripping Trevor's trunk with her claws. Cressida wrapped her arms around Riley's neck and squeezed Riley's back with her knees as Riley climbed up to the end of the highest branch.

"Get ready!" Riley called, springing forward into the air. As they soared through the sky, they passed right under the cloud. Cressida reached up and grabbed the rainbow. It felt soft and slippery in her hand, like a long silk scarf. As Cressida clung to the rainbow, Riley glided downward and landed gracefully on the ground.

"Thank you!" Cressida said, sliding off Riley.

"My pleasure!" Riley replied. Then she

slunk back over to Trevor, scaled his trunk once more, and lay down on one of his biggest branches. "I sure have missed my favorite perch today," she purred, yawning and closing her eyes.

Cressida spread out the rainbow on the ground. The ribbons of color shimmered, as though they were made of wet paint.

"Do you know what I'm supposed to do next?" Cressida asked the unicorns.

Sunbeam shrugged.

Breeze tilted her head to one side and said, "I have no idea."

"I guess they didn't teach you this part in school," Prism said.

Cressida laughed. "We'll just have to figure it out ourselves," she said, pulling the paintbrush from her smock pocket. It hummed and glowed in her hand. She touched the brush to the red stripe on the rainbow. Glittery light swirled around her as the paintbrush filled with red. Cressida touched the bristles to the ground, and five blades of grass turned from clear to a bright, vibrant red. Next, she tapped the brush against Trevor. A swirl of red flowered on his otherwise clear bark.

Cressida smiled with delight. But then she heard a sniffling noise. She turned and saw tears streaming down Prism's face.

"What's wrong?" Cressida asked, surprised her unicorn friend wasn't thrilled to see color returning to the Valley of Light.

"I'm glad and grateful you found the

rainbow," Prism sniffled, "but at this rate, it will take weeks to repaint the whole valley."

Breeze furrowed her brow. "I'd offer to help, but I don't even have a paintbrush."

"If we're going to be here for a long time, maybe I should go get some snacks," suggested Sunbeam.

Cressida paused. Prism was right that if Cressida repainted the Valley of Light all by herself, it might take weeks—and maybe even months—to restore the valley's colors. What they needed, Cressida thought, were more painters. And that's when she remembered Titania's offer to help. "Prism," Cressida said, "would you ask Titania if she and the fairies might be willing to come help paint?"

Before Prism could respond, a familiar voice behind Cressida and the unicorns said, "Of course we would!"

Cressida turned and saw Titania fluttering her wings and holding a giant paintbrush. Behind her hovered more fairies than Cressida could count, each holding a paintbrush as they beat their wings. "We felt a huge gust of wind—so strong it could only have come from Princess Breeze—and then we saw the rainbow hanging from a rain cloud in the distance. That's when we all grabbed our paintbrushes and rushed over to you. Nothing would make us happier than to help paint the Valley of Light."

A grin spread across Prism's face. "Thank you," she said.

Titania turned to the fairies behind her. "Fill up your paintbrushes!" she called out.

The fairies cheered and laughed as they fluttered over to the rainbow and touched their brushes to the ribbons of red, orange, yellow, green, blue, and purple. Their brushes hummed as the fairies then spread out across the valley and began to paint.

Soon, violet and lemon-yellow wild-flowers swayed in the wind. Red, orange, yellow, green, blue, and purple stripes cascaded down the Rainbow Cats' backs. They looked, Cressida realized, just like

the cat on her shirt. Curly red, turquoise, magenta, and mint-green lines danced up the trees' trunks. Fuchsia and maroon fish leaped from swirls of mustard-yellow and light orange river water. Blades of grass in every color Cressida could imagine shimmered in the sunlight.

Cressida looked over at Prism, who was still completely see-through. Though the unicorn looked thrilled and relieved to see the color returning so rapidly to the Valley of Light, Cressida could tell her friend felt anxious to have her magic working again. "Would you like me to paint you and your amethyst now?" Cressida asked.

"Yes!" cried Prism, dancing with excitement. "I can't wait to be back in my very own purple coat, with a magic gemstone that actually works!"

"I bet!" Cressida said, dipping her paintbrush into the rainbow's purple stripe and touching the bristles to Prism. Soon, Prism's coat was a glossy lavender, her mane and tail shone like purple silk, her horn and hooves glimmered like purple foil. Cressida pressed her paintbrush against Prism's gemstone. Purple glittery light swirled around the amethyst, and then it shimmered a vibrant purple.

"Marvelous!" Titania exclaimed, admiring Cressida's work. And then the fairy queen dipped her brush into the rainbow's green stripe and painted Prism's ribbon.

"I have my magic back!" Prism sang as she danced in a circle. "Now I can make art again! Does anyone have any paper?"

"I do!" said Roxy, and she darted away and returned with a large, blank piece of paper in her mouth. She put it down in a patch of green, orange, and purple moss in front of Prism.

"Thank you!" Prism said.

Next, the unicorn pointed her horn toward the paper. Her amethyst shimmered. And then a beam of glittery purple light shot from her horn. Suddenly, a blob that included every color of the rainbow appeared on the paper. It looked, Cressida thought, a little bit like a rainbow puddle. Prism kept shooting purple light at the paper, and Cressida watched as the blob slowly took the shape of a human. By the time Prism was done, Cressida realized she had just painted a girl with bright red hair, green skin, purple eyes, blue ears, and a yellow nose.

"It's you!" Prism said. "Do you like it?"

"I love it!" Cressida said.

"I've been wanting to paint you ever since you told me you painted a picture of me!" Prism said. "Maybe you could even take it home with you?"

"Really?" Cressida asked, imagining putting the picture up on the wall of her room, right next to the pictures of Sunbeam, Flash, Bloom, and Prism.

"It's my gift to you," Prism said. "Thank you for helping to restore all the color to the Valley of Light and for getting my magic back. I love creating art more than anything else in the whole world, and it was miserable not to be able to do what I love."

"Thank you so very much," Cressida said. She pulled the paper off the mossy ground, rolled it up, and put it in her back pocket.

"I know you probably need to get home," Prism said, "but I'm so glad you could see the Valley of Light in full color."

"Me too," Cressida said, and she put her arm around Prism. "And I want you to know that I don't think your purple coat is boring at all. I'm glad to see you looking like yourself again."

"Well, thank you," Prism said, blushing.

"I agree," Breeze said. "I like you just the way you are. And I bet you're relieved you can make art again."

"I sure am," Prism said.

Just then, Cressida's stomach growled. And she thought about her math homework, still in her backpack. "I've had so much fun today," Cressida said, "but I think I'd better get home. I can't wait to put your painting up on my bedroom wall. And I'm ready to get started on my homework."

"Homework?" Prism said, looking confused. "Is that something else related to school?"

"It sure is," Cressida said.

Prism smiled and nodded. “Well, I don’t know what we’d do without you, Cressida,” she said. “Please come back soon.”

“Yes,” said Breeze, “please do.”

“I promise I will,” Cressida said. And she pulled the magic, old-fashioned key out of her pocket and said, “Take me home, please.”

Immediately, the Valley of Light began to spin into a rainbow-colored blur before everything went pitch black. Cressida felt the wonderful sensation of flying straight up into the air. She giggled. Soon, she found herself sitting on the forest floor, under the oak tree with the magic keyhole. For a moment, the woods spun. And then, everything was still.

Cressida smiled. She stood and looked down. Her rainbow smock and the magic paintbrush were gone, and her sneakers were silver again. She touched her head. The dandelion wreath was gone, too. But she felt something in her back pocket: the rolled-up picture of her that Prism had painted. She touched it and smiled, eager to hang it next to the other paintings on her bedroom wall. And then she skipped home, the pink lights on her sneakers blinking merrily.

Unicorn Princesses

BREEZE'S BLAST

Chapter One

In the top tower of Spiral Palace, Ernest, the wizard-lizard, stared at his bookshelf. He tilted his scaly green head to one side and his pointy hat almost toppled off. "Hmm," he said. "What book of spells should I study ncxt? *Magic Storms and Other Bewitched Weather*? No, the unicorn princesses wouldn't like that much. *Enchanted Bangs and Conjured Crashes*? Nope, too loud. What about—"

Before he could finish his sentence, a loud thumping on the door interrupted him. "Come in!" he called out, straightening his hat and cloak.

The wooden door creaked open, and a red dragon wearing a white chef's hat and apron entered. "Good morning, Ernest!" the dragon boomed. His flame-colored eyes glimmered, and blue smoke puffed from his nostrils. In one clawed hand he held eight bulbs of garlic.

"Hello, Drew," Ernest said, smiling eagerly. "Can I help you with something?"

"You sure can!" Drew bellowed. "We dragons down in the palace kitchen were wondering if you might provide us with some magical assistance."

"With pleasure!" Ernest said, jumping with glee.

"Fantastic," Drew said as threads of smoke rose from his nose. "Could you turn these bulbs of garlic into eight large cooking vats? We're preparing to make the Blast Feast for Princess Breeze, but none of our usual pots are big enough."

"I know just the right book of spells!" Ernest exclaimed. He grabbed a thin red book entitled *Magic in the Kitchen* and flipped to a page that said, in large letters across

the top, "Big Pots, Large Pans, Giant Vats, and Humongous Cauldrons."

"Thank you!" Drew said, and he set the garlic bulbs down on Ernest's table.

"I'm sure I can do this one perfectly on the first try," Ernest said. He read over the spell several times, mouthing the words silently. Then he stepped up to his table, grabbed his magic wand from his cloak pocket, and lifted it into the air. He took a deep breath before he chanted, "Cookily Slookily Stockily Stew! Garlic Starlic Smarlic Smew! Make Eight Bats for a Tasty Brew!"

Ernest waited. The bulbs of garlic didn't spin or jump or quiver. Instead, thunder rumbled. Ernest scratched his head. "Oh dear," Ernest said. "I'm not sure why that didn't work."

"Well," Drew said, "I'm not a wizard, so I don't know for sure, but I think it's because you said 'bats' instead of 'vats.' "

"Oh dear!" Ernest said again, slapping his hand to his forehead. Ernest turned and looked out the window just as eight bolts of silver lightning tore through the sky right above a distant meadow.

Drew shrugged. "We all make mistakes," he said. "I usually have to try a recipe five or six times before I get it right."

"Hopefully Princess Breeze won't notice anything is amiss before the Blast," Ernest said. Then he turned toward the garlic, cleared his throat, lifted his wand, and chanted, "Cookily Slookily Stockily Stew! Garlic Starlic Smarlic Smew! Make Eight Vats for a Tasty Brew!"

The bulbs of garlic spun around, faster and faster. Then, with a swirl of wind and a bright flash of light, the garlic vanished, and a tower of eight enormous silver vats appeared by the door.

"Marvelous!" Drew boomed, and a huge cloud of smoke came out of his nose. "I'm impressed you got it on the second try. Well done!"

"Thank you," Ernest said, blushing.

Drew turned to the stack of vats and hoisted two off the top. "These are heavy!

I'll take these down to the kitchen, and then I'll come back and get the rest. Thanks again for your help!" The dragon, with one arm wrapped around each vat, lumbered out of the room.

Chapter Two

Early one Saturday morning, Cressida Jenkins watched the willow trees in her backyard bend and sway in the wind, and she decided to build her first-ever homemade kite.

While her parents drank coffee and talked in the kitchen, Cressida collected sticks, scissors, tape, and markers from her desk drawer. She found a pink plastic bag under the kitchen sink and then sat down with her supplies on the living room floor. Corey, her older brother, lay on the couch drinking orange juice and reading *All About Bats*, a book he had gotten from their grandmother for his birthday.

Cressida cut the plastic bag into a large diamond. She arranged the sticks into a cross and taped them to the diamond. Next, she used the markers to decorate the pink plastic with pictures of the seven unicorn princesses Cressida had befriended: yellow Sunbeam, silver Flash, green Bloom, purple Prism, blue Breeze, black Moon, and orange Firefly.

Corey glanced at Cressida's kite and rolled his eyes. "Are you ever going to stop

being obsessed with unicorns?" he asked. "Bats are much better. For one thing, they're actually real. And, they can fly. Did you know they sleep all day and hunt mosquitoes and other insects all night? I bet unicorns, even if they were real, couldn't do that."

Cressida shrugged. She had much better things to do—like fly her kite—than argue with her brother. "I like unicorns *and* bats," she said as she used a light blue marker to put the final touches on Breeze's mane and tail.

Little did Corey know that not only were unicorns just as real as bats, but that any time she wanted to, Cressida could visit the Rainbow Realm—a magical land ruled by the unicorn princesses. To travel there, all she had to do was push a special key into a secret hole in the base of a giant oak tree in the woods behind their house.

"Why are the unicorns wearing those strange things around their necks?" Corey asked, frowning as he studied her kite.

"They're magic necklaces," Cressida explained. Just like the real princess unicorns, each of the unicorns Cressida had drawn wore a magic gemstone that hung from a colored ribbon.

Corey sighed. "Magic isn't real, either," he said.

Cressida smiled mysteriously. "That's what you think," she replied, not bothering to look up. When her grandmother had visited for Corey's birthday, she'd given Cressida a set of permanent markers in metallic shades. Now, Cressida used the gold one to color in Sunbeam's hooves and horn.

"Things that are real can be pretty amazing," Corey said, looking down at his open book. "Did you know that the biggest kind of bats have a wingspan of up to six feet? Can you imagine a bat that big?"

"That's pretty neat," Cressida said, pausing to imagine a bat with a wingspan that was just as long as her father was tall.

"Maybe I'll make a gigantic bat kite after I finish this book," Corey said.

"I'll help you with it," Cressida said.

Then, as Corey continued to read,

Cressida drew a rainbow that arched over the unicorn princesses.

Now the only thing left to do before she could fly her kite was to make it a tail. Cressida stood up and skipped across the living room, down the hall, and into her bedroom. She pulled her art supply bin off her shelves. And just as she began to rummage through a mess of paints, markers, crayons, yarn, stickers, glue, tape, sequins, and beads, she heard a high, tinkling noise.

Cressida grinned and leaped across the room to her bedside table. She opened the drawer and pulled out an old-fashioned key with a crystal ball handle. The ball glowed bright pink as the key continued to make the tinkling noise. It was the special signal the unicorns used to invite her to visit them in the Rainbow Realm!

Cressida, who was still wearing her green unicorn pajamas, changed into a pair of jeans, a teal T-shirt with a picture of a kite with a rainbow tail, and her favorite shoes: a pair of silver unicorn sneakers. She especially loved them because they had pink lights that blinked whenever she walked, ran, or jumped.

With the key safely stowed in the back pocket of her jeans, Cressida dashed out of her room and sprinted to the back door.

"Where are you going in such a hurry?" Corey called out. "And aren't you going to take your kite?"

"I'll be right back," Cressida said as she

stepped outside. "I'm just going for a quick walk in the woods before I try to fly it."

"Have fun," Cressida's father called from the kitchen.

Fortunately, time in the human world froze while Cressida was in the Rainbow Realm, so even if she spent hours with the unicorns, Corey and her parents would think she'd been gone only a few minutes.

Cressida ran through her backyard and turned onto her favorite path in the woods behind her house. When she came to the giant oak, she kneeled down and found the tiny hole in the base of the tree. Her heart thundered with excitement as she pushed the key into the hole. The forest began to spin, turning into a whirl of brown and green, and then everything turned pitch black. Suddenly Cressida felt as though she were falling through space. Then, with a gentle thud, she landed on something soft. For a moment, all she could see was a blur of white, pink, and purple. But when the room stopped spinning, Cressida found

herself sitting on a lavender armchair in the front hall of Spiral Palace, the unicorns' white, sparkling, horn-shaped home.

Crystal chandeliers shimmered from the ceiling. Light poured in through the windows, as pink, purple, and silver curtains fluttered in the breeze. Cressida looked all around the room for her unicorn friends, but the unicorn-size velvet couches and chairs were empty.

"Hello?" Cressida called out, standing up and walking to the center of the room. "Is anyone here?"

Then she heard a clattering of hooves in the hallway. In a few seconds, all seven unicorn princesses trotted up to Cressida.

Chapter Three

Breeze danced over to Cressida and sang out, "Yippee! You're here! We were trying to sneak into the palace kitchen to see what the dragons are cooking, but they caught us!" Her magic gemstone—an aquamarine—hung from an orange ribbon around her neck and glittered in the light of the chandeliers. From her other trips to the Rainbow Realm,

Cressida knew Breeze's magic power was to create gusts of blue wind.

"My human girl is back!" Sunbeam sang out, clicking her gold hooves together.

"We're so glad you could come," Flash said, swishing her silver tail.

Bloom and Prism reared up with excitement. And Firefly winked at Cressida.

The only unicorn who didn't look happy was Moon, who stood apart from her sisters and stared worriedly at her shiny black hooves.

Cressida wanted to ask Moon what was wrong, but before she could, Breeze gushed, "We invited you here for our annual Windy Meadows Blast. It's my favorite day of the year, and I'm so excited I can't stand still."

Breeze trotted backward in circles around Cressida. "You're just in time to come to the Windy Meadows to help me prepare for the Blast. Will you join me? Please!"

Cressida giggled. "Of course I will," she said. "But what is the Blast?"

"It's a special day when all my sisters and I ride huge kites up into the clouds," Breeze explained. "Afterwards, the dragons cook us a fantastic feast. We want you to be the first human girl to ride up into the clouds with us."

"I'd love that," Cressida said. Flying into the clouds on a kite with seven unicorns sounded like more fun than almost anything else Cressida could imagine doing that morning.

Moon frowned and sighed loudly. Cressida opened her mouth to ask Moon what was wrong, but before she could speak, a red dragon wearing a puffy white hat and apron appeared. He whistled as he carried two enormous metal vats through the palace's front room and down a hallway that led to the kitchen. Cressida knew from her first visit to the Rainbow Realm that the dragons were chefs who cooked the unicorns' food with their fiery breath.

"Won't you please tell us what you're making for the Blast feast?" Breeze called out when she saw the dragon.

The dragon laughed, and blue smoke poured from his nostrils. "No chance!" he chortled. "It's a secret. But you're going to love it! We've been practicing the recipes for weeks. Now, if you'll excuse me, I need to put these vats in the kitchen and go get the rest of the ones Ernest made for me." With that, he disappeared down the hall, his enormous, spiked tale dragging behind him.

"I'm already hungry for the Blast feast," Breeze said. "I skipped breakfast so I'd have extra room."

"Me too!" Sunbeam and Flash said at once.

Flash turned to Sunbeam and narrowed her eyes. "*You* did?" she asked. "That doesn't sound like you."

Sunbeam blushed. "Well, okay, I had a little bit of breakfast," she admitted.

"I started to get cranky because I was hungry and I ate some roinkleberries. Well, a lot of roinkleberries. And some mushrooms. And an avocado. But trust me, I'm already hungry for the feast!"

"Prism, Firefly, and I meant to just have a small breakfast," Bloom said, smiling self-consciously, "but then we saw a cluster of huge, perfectly ripe froyananas hanging from a tree. And, well, we couldn't resist!" Cressida's stomach turned. When she had visited Bloom's domain, the Enchanted Garden, she had taken one bite of a froyanana only to discover it tasted like a terrible mix of pickles, marshmallows, tomatoes, and tuna fish.

Prism nodded. "They were amazing!

But by the time the dragons have cooked their feast, I'm sure we'll be hungry."

"Definitely," Firefly added. "I can't wait for all of us to fly up into the sky together."

Moon glanced up, and Cressida could see the unicorn's eyes had filled with tears.

"What's wrong, Moon?" Cressida asked.

Moon sniffled. "I'm not coming to the Blast this year, or ever again," she said. "I'm too scared."

"Oh no," Flash whispered to Cressida. "Moon fell off her kite last year, and although she didn't get hurt, she's been terrified of this year's Blast ever since."

Cressida nodded. She certainly understood what it felt like to be scared after an accident—once, she had fallen off a playground swing, and she hadn't wanted to go anywhere near that swing set, or even that park, afterward. Later, when she felt ready, she had returned to the park with her friends Gillian and Eleanor, and she had even tried—and enjoyed—swinging. But it had taken her awhile to feel like swinging again.

Breeze looked at Moon and said, "I know you're scared, but you have to come to the Blast. It won't be any fun without you."

"I'm sure you won't fall off again this year," Sunbeam said.

Moon shook her head, and more tears streamed down her cheeks.

"Come on, Moon," Prism said. "We all want you to fly with us."

"I told you, I'm not coming," Moon said. "Would you please listen to me? Stop trying to make me do something I don't want to do!" With that, she turned and galloped down the hallway.

Breeze frowned. "I feel bad for Moon, but I just really hope she changes her mind," she said. "The Blast won't be any fun without all of us there, flying together."

"I'll go talk to her as soon as you and Cressida leave for the Windy Meadows to prepare for the Blast," Flash said. "Don't worry! I'm sure I can convince her to come fly with us."

"Thank you, Flash!" Breeze said, and her eyes lit back up with excitement. She turned to Cressida. "Are you ready to come with me to the Windy Meadows? I can't wait to show you around."

"Absolutely!" Cressida said. Though she felt excited to visit the Windy Meadows, she also felt worried about Moon. She hoped the other unicorns would be able to comfort their sister.

"What are we waiting for? Let's go!" Breeze called out, kneeling down. But just as Cressida started to climb onto Breeze's back, a high, nasal voice cried, "Hold on! Wait!" And then Cressida heard the unmistakable sound of Ernest, the wizard-lizard, running as fast as his feet could carry him down the hall and toward the front room of the palace.

"Hello, Ernest!" Cressida said, giggling.

"Before you go," Ernest said, "I have a present for you! I've been practicing this spell for the past hour, and I'm absolutely sure I've finally gotten it right!"

Cressida smiled and braced herself for a magical mishap. Every time she came to the Rainbow Realm, Ernest got at least one spell wrong.

The wizard-lizard took a deep breath. He pulled his wand from his cloak. And then he chanted, "Safety Sequiny Satiny Bright! Make a Magic Grape for Cressida's Flight!"

A gust of wind swirled around Cressida.

And then she felt something cool, wet, and mushy against her skin. She looked down and laughed to see that she was inside a giant, bright blue, sequin-covered grape. Only her head stuck out from the top.

"Oh dear!" Ernest exclaimed.

The giant grape, with Cressida inside it, began to roll forward. "Yikes!" Cressida said as Breeze and Bloom rushed over and used their hooves to keep her upright.

"Oops," Ernest said. "When I was practicing upstairs, I kept accidentally making apes. And one time I even made a roll of tape. But a grape is something new. Hold on. Oh dear!"

Ernest scratched his head. He raised his wand. And he chanted, "Gibbledy Globbledy Gobbledy Goo! Trade in this Grape for a Cape of Blue!"

More wind swirled around Cressida, and, to her relief, the giant grape vanished and now both her feet were firmly planted on the ground. When she looked down, she saw she was wearing a long, bright turquoise, sequined cape.

"Wow! I love it!" Cressida said, twirling around so the cape billowed.

Ernest grinned with delight. "It's a special magic cape," he explained. "If you fall off your kite, it will keep you from getting hurt when you land on the ground. It came out just a little larger than I expected. I hope you don't mind."

"It's absolutely perfect. Thank you, Ernest," Cressida said. Then she looked at Breeze. "How do I look?" she asked.

"Ready to fly!" Breeze exclaimed.

Cressida looked at her reflection on the marble floor and smiled: she thought she looked just like a superhero. She made a fist and extended her hand up into the air, as though she were about to fly up into the sky.

"What are you doing?" asked Flash.

"I'm pretending to be a superhero!" Cressida said.

"A superhero?" Breeze asked. "What's that?"

"Well," Cressida said, "a superhero is a human with magic powers who solves problems. They aren't real, but it's fun to pretend to be one."

"Huh," Breeze and Sunbeam said at the same time.

Then Breeze shrugged and said, "Let's go!" She kneeled down, and Cressida climbed onto her back.

Breeze turned toward the other unicorn princesses and said, "We'll see you in the Windy Meadows. Make sure you bring Moon!" And with Cressida on her back she raced out the palace's front door.

Chapter Four

Cressida gripped Breeze's silky, light blue mane as the unicorn raced along the path of clear stones that led away from Spiral Palace and into the surrounding forest. Cressida turned, and for a few seconds she watched the tall, glittering white palace, shaped like a unicorn horn, fade into the distance.

"The only thing we really need to do to

get ready for the Blast is to make sure the kites are lined up and ready to fly," Breeze said, jumping playfully as she galloped. "That means we have time for me to show you my two very favorite parts of the Windy Meadows first."

"What are they?" Cressida asked, feeling her heart beat with excitement.

"It's a surprise!" Breeze sang out as she turned down a narrow path that cut through a thicket of pine trees.

"I can't wait," Cressida said, grinning. She loved surprises, and the Rainbow Realm was always full of surprises that were even better than anything she could imagine.

Breeze followed the path across a patch of blue mushrooms, up a fern-covered hill, and over to a grove of willow trees.

"We're almost there!" Breeze said. "Close your eyes!"

Cressida squeezed her eyes shut as Breeze turned sharply to the right, slowed down, and stopped. "Okay! You can look now," the unicorn said.

When Cressida opened her eyes, she saw that she and Breeze were standing right in the middle of a meadow so full of large orange ball-shaped flowers that she could hardly see any grass.

"Welcome to the Windy Meadows!" Breeze said, kneeling down as Cressida slid off her back. "This meadow is just our first stop. It's called the Meadow of Metamorflowers."

"Are these metamorflowers?" Cressida asked, looking more closely at the flowers. As they brushed against Cressida's knees and the bottom of her cape, she noticed each orange ball was made of what looked like hundreds of tiny feather-shaped petals.

"Not only are they metamorflowers," Breeze said, shuffling her hooves with excitement, "but they're *magic* metamorflowers. I'll show you!"

The unicorn pointed her blue horn toward the sky. The aquamarine on her ribbon necklace shimmered. Glittery light

shot from her horn. And then a blue, comet-shaped gust of wind appeared. First, it bolted straight up into the air and did three somersaults. Then it plunged down to the flowers, where it circled Breeze and Cressida, faster and faster, until Cressida felt as though she were in the center of a small tornado. Thousands of orange petals lifted off the flowers' stems and into the air, and soon Cressida felt as though she were standing in an orange blizzard.

Then the petals fluttered into a large pile right in front of Cressida's feet and Breeze's hooves. Cressida reached down and grabbed a handful of petals. To her surprise, they stuck together, almost like clay or snow.

"Now watch this!" Breeze said, and she used her hooves to roll a clump of petals into what looked like a snake. Then, with her nose, she tossed it upward. To Cressida's amazement, in the air, it transformed into what looked like a real orange snake, slithering above them.

"Yikes!" Cressida said, jumping backward.

"Don't worry," Breeze said, laughing. "It can't hurt you!"

As Cressida watched, fascinated and a little scared, the snake wiggled, slid, and hissed. And then, as suddenly as it had seemed to come alive, the snake turned back to a shower of petals that fluttered to the ground.

"My sisters and I can spend hours here at a time," Breeze said. "The only problem is that since my sisters and I have hooves, the only things we can do are roll and flatten the petals. Since there aren't very many animals that look like pancakes, we end up making a lot of snakes, eels, and worms. And once I even managed a caterpillar." Breeze's eyes filled with excitement. "But I bet, since you have fingers and a thumb, you could make all kinds of animals. Try it!"

Cressida picked up two handfuls of petals and smushed them together. Then, she shaped the petals into a rabbit with long ears, large paws, and a small, fluffy-looking tail.

"Throw it into the air!" Breeze said, bounding from side to side.

Cressida tossed it up, and the rabbit seemed to come alive, hopping, sniffing, and scratching its ears.

Then, right in the middle of a jump, it

fell apart, and the petals fluttered to the ground.

"Wow!" Cressida said, laughing with delight as she grabbed more petals and sculpted a cheetah. "This is much more fun than regular modeling clay!" After she used her fingernail to give the cat's body spots, she launched it into the air and watched as it sprinted in circles over her head.

"That cheetah is an even faster runner than Flash," Breeze said with wide eyes. Flash's magic power was to run so fast that lightning bolts crackled from her horn and hooves.

After the cheetah turned into a shower of petals, Cressida made an eagle that soared and swooped, an elephant that swung its trunk, a monkey that hung from its tail, and an alligator that snapped its jaws as it crept forward. Breeze rolled out five more snakes, three eels, and two earthworms.

"Guess what? I have an idea for an animal we could make together," Cressida said.

"What is it?" Breeze asked, her eyes lighting up.

"It's a surprise," Cressida said, winking. "But if you make eight snakes, I'll make the rest."

As Breeze got to work rolling clumps of petals, Cressida used her hands to sculpt an elongated ball with eyes and a mouth.

Then she attached Breeze's snakes to the ball.

"An octopus!" Breeze exclaimed. "What a great idea!"

Cressida giggled and threw the octopus into the air. It glided above them, waving its tentacles as though it were underwater. And then it fell apart.

Just as Cressida was about to suggest they make a giant spider together in the same way, Breeze sighed and said, "This has been so much fun, but I think we'd better stop and tidy up. I want to make sure there's time to show you one more thing before we check on the kites."

"Of course," Cressida said, feeling both disappointed to leave and curious about what else Breeze wanted to show her. "How can I help tidy up?"

"Thanks so much for offering," Breeze said, "but I always just use magic to clean up the petals. Watch this!" She pointed her horn toward the sky. The aquamarine on her ribbon shimmered as glittery light shot from her horn. A gust of blue wind swirled around Cressida and Breeze. And the petals lifted into the air and returned to their stems, re-forming into the ball-shaped flowers Cressida had seen when they first arrived at the meadow. A gentle breeze riffled through the flowers, and once again they brushed against her knees and the bottom of her cape.

"Wow! That's the quickest cleaning job

I've ever seen," Cressida said, wishing she could use magic to clean her room.

Breeze kneeled down. "Climb on up," she said. "Our next stop is the Meadow of Melodies."

Chapter Five

With Cressida on her back, Breeze trotted under a canopy of green leafy elms and into another meadow, this one dotted with trees and shrubs. A gentle breeze blew, and Cressida heard faint, high-pitched music that reminded her of the sound her key to the Rainbow Realm made when the unicorns invited her to visit. Cressida looked at the

trees and shrubs more carefully and saw that wind chimes hung from nearly every branch. Some were metal and some were wood. The large wind chimes played lower notes, while the small ones played high-pitched music.

Breeze kneeled, and Cressida slid to the ground.

"What song would you like to hear?" Breeze asked, grinning excitedly.

"Hmm," Cressida said, trying to think of a song Breeze might know.

But before she could answer, Breeze said, "How about 'Twinkle, Twinkle, Little Star'?"

Cressida smiled. When she was younger,

that had been one of her favorite songs. "Sure!" she said.

"I have to admit, it's my favorite song," Breeze said, blushing. Then she pointed her horn to the sky. Her aquamarine shimmered. Glittery light shot from her horn, and a star-shaped gust of blue wind appeared, this one smaller and gentler than the one that had appeared in the Meadow of Metamorflowers. The gust danced through the trees and shrubs, and as the branches swayed, Cressida heard the most beautiful rendition of "Twinkle, Twinkle, Little Star" she could have imagined. No wonder it was Breeze's favorite song, she thought. Cressida smiled with delight as the wind chimes played the song over and over, each time a little more faintly, as the gust lost its strength.

"That's really neat," Cressida said.

"I know!" Breeze said. "And now, I think we'd really better go make sure the kites are ready. When I fed them breakfast this morning, they promised they would be all lined up by now. But sometimes they get distracted by an especially good gust of wind, and they're late."

"Wait a minute," Cressida said, smiling with delight. "The kites are alive?" She wasn't sure why she was so surprised. After all, on other visits to the Rainbow Realm, she had met boulders and dunes that talked. And yet, the idea of a talking, laughing, live kite especially delighted her.

"Of course they're alive," said Breeze. "And not only are they alive, but they're a little bit mischievous and wild. They love to fly upside down and in circles in the air. That's why Moon fell off during last year's Blast. Her kite, Kevin, was in an especially rambunctious mood, and he tried to fly too fast." Cressida nodded. Worry flashed across Breeze's face. "I sure do hope Flash has convinced Moon to participate in the Blast by now. Anyway," the unicorn said, her face brightening, "come this way! The kites always line up in the Monarch Meadow."

"The Monarch Meadow?" Cressida asked as they walked along a row of windmills. "Like the butterfly?" In school, they had learned the names of different butterflies, including monarchs, which were orange with black markings.

"Exactly!" Breeze said, looking impressed.

Cressida followed Breeze down a hill, through a cluster of willow trees, and into a meadow teeming with wildflowers and orange-and-black butterflies. In the middle of all the butterflies and wildflowers were eight of the biggest, bluest kites she had ever seen. And on top of each one slept a silver, furry animal that was twice the size of a unicorn. Each animal had shiny, folded wings and large, round ears.

"What are those?" Breeze asked, furrowing her brow.

“Are they giant flying mice?” Cressida asked, walking toward one. When she looked more closely, she saw two sharp teeth poking out from the animal’s mouth. “I think they’re huge bats,” Cressida said. She remembered that Corey had told her that very morning that bats sleep all day and search for food at night. “They must be sleeping because it’s daytime.”

"Huge bats?" Breeze said, looking panicked. "Where did those come from?"

But before Cressida could suggest that one of Ernest's accidental spells might be to blame, a kite called out, "Is that you, Princess Breeze?"

Another said, "Help! We can't get up!"

"Plus, it's awfully hot under here," a third voice added.

"It's me!" called out Breeze. "What happened?"

"Well," one of the kites said, "we had just finished practicing some of our stunts and tricks. And then we were lining up for the Blast when, all of a sudden, lightning flashed. There was an even stronger gust of wind than usual, and the next thing we knew, there was a giant bat sleeping on each of us."

"How will we get them off?" Breeze asked Cressida.

"Well," Cressida said, "Maybe we should start by just asking them to leave."

"Will you do it?" Breeze asked, looking nervous. "I've always been a little afraid of bats. And these are the biggest bats I've ever seen."

"Sure," Cressida said. She walked closer to the bats. "Excuse me," she said. The bats didn't even stir. "Excuse me!" she called out again, this time much louder. The bats blinked and yawned. "I'm sorry to wake you, but I'm wondering if you might sleep somewhere else. Princess Breeze needs these kites."

The bat closest to Cressida frowned. "The trouble," the bat squeaked, "is that it is daytime and we are all very sleepy."

"I don't think," another bat squeaked, "that there is any way that we can get up right now. You'll have to wait until it's nighttime."

"Sorry!" a third bat squeaked.

And with that, all eight bats yawned, closed their eyes, and began to snore.

"Oh no," Breeze said. "Could you possibly try pushing them off the kites?" Cressida looked again at the bats. "I think they're probably too heavy," she said.

Breeze looked as though she might start crying. "Would you be willing to try, just in case it works?" Breeze asked. "I don't know what I'll do if we have to cancel the Blast. All the dragons' hard work cooking our feast would go to waste."

"Okay," Cressida said. "It won't hurt to try!" She walked up to the smallest bat, took a deep breath, and used both hands to push as hard as she could on his back. The bat's fur felt soft against her hands, like a rabbit's. As Cressida shoved with all her might, the bat didn't even stir or open his eyes, let alone move. It would have been easier, she thought, to push a car.

She dropped her arms and walked back to Breeze. "I'm sorry, but they're just too heavy," Cressida said. "But I have another idea. What if you created a gust of wind strong enough to blow them off the kites?"

Breeze smiled hopefully. "Good idea! I'll try it!" she said. Glittery light shot from her horn just before a giant, comet-shaped gust of wind appeared. It bolted over to the bats, blowing hard against their heads, their bodies, and their folded wings. Some of the bats grunted and stretched. But they still didn't wake up, let alone roll off the kites.

"Oh no!" Breeze said, as the wind died down. "That was my very strongest gust of wind ever." The unicorn's top lip quivered. "What if we have to cancel the Blast?" Breeze asked as a tear rolled down her cheek.

Cressida turned, put her arms around Breeze, and said, “There must be a way to get the bats off the kites before the Blast. Let me just think for a moment.”

And then Cressida had an idea. She jumped up and down with excitement. “I think I know what to do! But we’re going to need to get Moon to help us.”

“Let’s go back to the palace and get her,” Breeze said. “I’ll bet Flash and my other sisters have convinced her to fly in the Blast by now!” The unicorn kneeled down, and Cressida climbed onto her back. As soon as Cressida had tightly gripped her mane, Breeze galloped back through the Windy Meadows toward Spiral Palace.

Chapter Six

With Cressida on her back, Breeze sped across the clear stones leading up to the front door of Spiral Palace. When they entered the front room, they found Sunbeam, Flash, Bloom, Prism, Moon, and Firefly standing in a circle.

"I'm not going," Moon said, shaking her head. "Last time was just too scary.

I never want to go anywhere near a giant kite again."

"What if we made sure to give you the calmest kite this year?" Sunbeam asked.

Moon shook her head.

"Would it help if I rode right next to you?" Flash asked.

Moon shook her head again.

"If you want, you could share a kite with me," Prism said. "Would that work?"

"No, but thank you for offering," Moon said.

"But if you don't fly with us, it will ruin the Blast," Bloom said. "It won't be any fun without you."

Moon began to cry, and she stomped

her front hooves angrily. "How many times do I have to tell you? I'm too scared. I'm not flying this year. Please stop trying to make me change my mind."

Breeze loudly cleared her throat, and her six sisters turned toward her. "We weren't expecting to see you back here right before the Blast," Flash said. "Is something wrong?"

"Yes," Breeze said. "When we got to the Windy Meadows, we discovered gigantic bats sleeping on the kites. Cressida tried to shove them off. And I tried to push them off with a gust of wind. But they were too big and heavy. I'm worried we'll have to cancel the Blast."

"There are *bats* on all the kites?" Moon asked, suddenly grinning. She looked absolutely delighted that the Blast might be canceled. Meanwhile, all the other unicorns' faces fell.

"Oh no!" Bloom and Prism said in unison.

"That's terrible," Firefly said.

"Sounds like Ernest made another mistake," Flash said, grimacing.

"What will we do?" Sunbeam asked.

"Well," Breeze said, "Cressida says she has one last idea."

All the unicorn princesses turned toward Cressida. She smiled and nodded. And then she said, "I do have a plan, but we'll need Moon's help."

Moon shook her head. "I'm sorry, but I have to admit I really want the Blast to be canceled. I still have bad dreams about the time I fell off my kite. I don't think I can help you."

Flash, Sunbeam, Bloom, Prism, Firefly, and Breeze all began to talk at once, trying to convince Moon to change her mind.

"Excuse me," Cressida said, politely but loudly. The unicorns stopped talking and turned toward her. Cressida remembered again how scared she had felt of swinging after she had fallen off her swing—and how much she wouldn't have liked anyone pushing her to swing again before she felt ready.

"Moon," Cressida said, "would you be

willing to help get the bats off the kites if your sisters agreed to stop trying to get you to fly in the Blast? Maybe you could just watch this year. Or, if that's too much, you could come back to stay in the palace during the Blast."

Moon thought for a moment, and then she nodded. "I know how much the Blast means to Breeze and my other sisters. If everyone would just stop putting pressure on me to fly, I'd help get the bats off the kites in any way I can." She looked at Breeze and continued, "I don't actually want you to have to cancel the Blast. It's just that I feel much too scared to ride a kite this year. And I don't like all of you

trying to convince me to do something I really don't want to do."

"That makes perfect sense to me," Cressida said to Moon, smiling reassuringly. Then she looked at the other unicorns. "I know all of you really want Moon to fly with you in the Blast, but she's saying she's not ready and it won't be fun for her. If she agrees to help get the bats off the kites, will you agree to stop trying to get her to fly?"

"Yes," Breeze said. "I'll be sad if Moon doesn't fly with us. But I don't want to cancel the Blast." She paused and thought for a moment. And then she looked at Moon. "I really do understand that you're just not ready to fly this year." The other unicorns nodded in agreement. "And I'm sorry we all kept trying to convince you to fly with us," Breeze continued. "I just always think things are more fun when we're all together. But Cressida is right. I should have listened when you said you were too scared."

"I forgive you," Moon said, grinning at

her sister. "Now let's go get those bats off the kites before it's too late!"

"Great," said Cressida. "If Breeze, Moon, and I go back to the Windy Meadows now, I think we'll be able to get the bats off the kites in time to hold the Blast."

Breeze kneeled down so Cressida could climb on her back, and, with Moon following right behind them, Breeze galloped out the front door. "See you very soon!" Breeze called.

Chapter Seven

"The first thing we need to do," Cressida said as she rode Breeze through the forest toward the Windy Meadows, "is pay another visit to the metamorflowers."

"Oh, I love the metamorflowers!" gushed Moon, who was galloping alongside Breeze. "My specialty is making extra-long earthworms!" Moon grinned, and Cressida felt relieved that the unicorn now seemed much happier.

"Cressida and I made an octopus together," Breeze said.

"It must be pretty neat to have fingers and thumbs," Moon said.

"It must be pretty neat to have magic powers," Cressida responded.

The three of them laughed.

Soon, Breeze, Moon, and Cressida stood in the center of the Meadow of Metamorflowers. Breeze kneeled down, and Cressida slid off her back and into the sea of orange flowers. "I bet you need me to make a pile of petals for you," Breeze said.

"Yes, please!" Cressida said.

"I can't wait to see what plan you have

in mind," Breeze said as she pointed her horn up into the sky. "You always have the most creative ideas." Her aquamarine shimmered. Glittery light shot from her horn. And a blue gust of wind swirled and danced through the meadow, sending all the orange petals into the air before they formed a pile at Cressida's feet.

Cressida picked up a clump of petals and rolled it into a ball. Then, she carefully began shaping the petals into a mosquito.

"What is that?" Moon asked, staring at the bug and scrunching up her nose.

"A giant mosquito," Cressida said.

"I don't think we have mosquitoes in the Rainbow Realm," Breeze said.

"I've never even heard of them," Moon said.

"That's lucky!" Cressida said, remembering a time she'd gone on a camping trip with her family and gotten covered in bites. "The real ones aren't any fun to have around. But I'm pretty sure mosquitoes made out of flower petals are harmless."

When Cressida finished sculpting the mosquito, she didn't throw it into the air to make it come alive. Instead, she turned to Breeze and asked, "Could I put this on your back?"

"Sure!" Breeze said.

"Thank you," Cressida said. With the mosquito safely balanced on Breeze's back,

Cressida got to work making seven more. She rested four on Breeze and four on Moon.

"Do you think," Cressida asked after she finished, "that if you both walked very carefully, you could get all the way to the bats without the mosquitoes falling off?"

"Definitely," Breeze said.

Moon nodded in agreement.

"I'll come back and tidy up the petals after the Blast," Breeze said. "I don't want the gust of wind I create to knock over and ruin your mosquitoes."

"Good idea!" Cressida said.

The three slowly made their way under the canopy of elms, across the Meadow of Melodies, through the willow trees, and back to the Monarch Meadow, where they found the gigantic bats still sleeping on the blue kites. Several orange-and-black butterflies perched on the bats, slowly opening and closing their wings.

"Before we wake up the bats, I think we'd better ask the butterflies to leave," Cressida said. "I don't want the bats to accidentally eat them." In school, Cressida had learned that monarch butterflies are poisonous to predators, and that their bright markings were supposed to warn lizards, birds, and frogs to stay away. She figured it wouldn't be good for the butterflies or the bats if the butterflies became an accidental snack.

"I'm glad you thought of that," Breeze said. And then she called out, "Attention! This is Princess Breeze. Monarch butterflies, could you please go to the Meadow of Melodies for a few minutes?"

All at once, the butterflies lifted off the bats and wildflowers and fluttered away.

Cressida looked at Moon. "Could you make the meadow pitch black?"

"Absolutely," Moon said, and took a deep

breath. She pointed her horn toward the enormous, snoring bats. The opal on her ribbon necklace shimmered. Black, glittery light shot out from her horn. And suddenly, the meadow was pitch black.

Within a few seconds, Cressida heard rustling. Then she heard yawning and giant bat wings unfolding and stretching.

"Is it night already?" a squeaky voice asked.

"I could have sworn I just went to bed a few hours ago," another voice squeaked.

"How strange! It feels like the sun just came up," piped a third.

"I guess we'd better look for some food," squeaked a fourth.

Cressida reached for the mosquitoes on

Breeze's back and quickly threw them into the air toward the bats. Then she tossed the mosquitoes on Moon's back in the same direction. In a few seconds, she heard the loud, high-pitched buzzing noise of eight large mosquitoes.

"I hear breakfast!" a voice squeaked, and then she heard the sound of eight giant bats flapping their wings, followed by very loud gulping and chewing noises.

"These are the strangest-tasting mosquitoes I've ever eaten," a voice squeaked.

"I swear they taste like flower petals," squeaked another bat.

"These are tasty! Let's go find some more!"

Soon the sound of flapping bat wings faded into the distance.

"Moon, I think you can make it light again now," Cressida said.

"Sure thing!" Moon said. And suddenly the Monarch Meadow was sunny again.

Cressida blinked and squinted as her eyes adjusted to the brightness. She stared into the distance and spotted the bats, which now, with their wings extended, looked even larger than she had imagined they were. She wished she could tell Corey that she had seen bats that were even bigger than the ones he had told her about. But she knew he would never believe her.

"Do you think they'll be able to find

somewhere to go back to sleep?" Cressida asked.

"Luckily, they're headed straight toward Firefly's domain, the Shimmering Caves," Breeze said. "I'll bet they'll find somewhere good to rest there."

The kites slowly stood up, balancing on their tails. They blinked their long, oval eyes and stretched their diamond-shaped bodies. Then, they began to chatter:

"Phew!"

"The bat lying on me smelled terrible!"

"And the one sitting on me was so heavy I couldn't even move my tail!"

"Plus, they snored so loudly!"

All the kites looked at each other and then at Cressida.

"Thank you!" they called out.

"Yes," Breeze said, looking at Cressida and Moon. "I feel so grateful to both of you. I'm very relieved I won't have to cancel the Blast."

"I was glad to help," Cressida said.

"Me too," said Moon. "I'm glad you'll be able to hold the Blast after all. And I'm excited to watch the rest of you fly up into the clouds."

Chapter Eight

As the kites stretched and jumped, Cressida spotted Flash, Sunbeam, Bloom, Prism, and Firefly trotting toward them.

"We're here and ready to fly!" exclaimed Flash.

"Yes," said Sunbeam. "We can't wait."

"Plus, I'm so hungry I could eat an entire froyanana tree, even the trunk and the leaves," Bloom said. Cressida heard a loud rumbling noise, and the unicorn blushed. "That's my stomach!" Bloom admitted. Cressida giggled.

"I can't wait for the dragon's special feast!" Prism said.

Cressida noticed that Moon was staring at a kite, almost as though she might want to climb onto it. Cressida decided not to say anything, though—she wanted to let Moon make her own decision, at her own pace, and without any pressure.

"Let's go!" Breeze said. "I can already smell the feast."

Cressida inhaled, and sure enough, she could smell food cooking. She looked all around for the dragons and their gigantic vats, but they were nowhere to be seen. "Where are the dragons?" she asked.

"Up in the sky!" Breeze said. "The clouds above this part of the Windy Meadows are special, magic clouds that we can stand and walk and bounce on."

Cressida's eyes widened with excitement. She had always wanted to walk and jump on clouds, but she had never thought that might be possible.

"Well," said Breeze, grinning at her sisters, "are you ready?"

"Yes!" cried Flash, Sunbeam, Bloom, Prism, and Firefly. Moon smiled and said, "I'll be here cheering you on."

While Cressida and Moon watched, the other unicorns raced over to the kites. Each unicorn stepped onto a kite so there were two left—one for Cressida, and one that would have been for Moon.

"Come on, Cressida!" Breeze called out. "Climb onto your kite!"

Cressida turned to Moon to say goodbye, but to her surprise, the unicorn had tears in her eyes. "I'll be right there!" Cressida called out to Breeze. Then she put her arms around Moon's neck. "You look like

you're having a hard time deciding what to do," Cressida said.

Moon nodded. "Now that I'm here looking at the kites, I really want to fly in the Blast. Look at how much fun my sisters are already having," she said. "And the dragon's feast is always the best meal I have all year. But I'm still terrified of falling off again. It was just so scary last year."

"I completely understand that," Cressida said. She looked over at the kites and then up at the clouds above them, where she knew the dragons were cooking. She realized she didn't feel so worried about falling off that she couldn't share the cape Ernest had made for her. After all, she wasn't afraid of heights, and she hadn't felt afraid the two other times she had soared through the sky in the Rainbow Realm—first on the boulders in Flash's domain, the Thunder Peaks, and then on the Rainbow Cats in Prism's domain, the Valley of Light.

"Moon," Cressida said, "after you left the front room of the palace this morning, Ernest gave me this special magic cape. It's supposed to keep me safe if I fall off a kite or a cloud. Would you like to share it with me? I don't want to put any pressure on you to get on a kite. But if you'd like to fly in the Blast, I'm sure it's big enough for both of us."

Moon's eyes widened. Relief, and then joy, washed over her face. "Really?" she asked, smiling.

"Really!" Cressida said.

"Are you sure?" Moon asked.

"I'm absolutely, positively sure!" Cressida said.

"I would love that," Moon said. She paused, and furrowed her brow. "But how will we share it?"

"Hmm," Cressida said. "That's a good

question." Even though the cape was roomy enough to fit over both of them, a single kite didn't look like it could safely hold both a girl and a unicorn.

"I can help with that," Breeze said, bounding over. "Just hold up the cape in front of you, and watch this!"

Cressida took off the cape and held it up. It was as wide as one of her bed sheets.

Breeze pointed her horn at the cape. Her aquamarine glittered. Blue, glittery light shot from her horn and a tiny but fierce gust of wind danced above the cape before it plunged downward, ripping the cape in two.

"Voila!" Breeze exclaimed. "Two magic capes!"

"Perfect," Cressida said, laughing. "Thank you, Breeze."

"My pleasure," Breeze said. She reared up with excitement and trotted back to her kite. Cressida draped one sequined cape over Moon's back and tied it around the unicorn's neck.

Then she put on the other one.

“How do I look?” Moon asked, twirling around with excitement.

“Ready to fly!” Cressida responded.

“I’m coming too!” Moon called out, and with her blue sequined cape flapping, she galloped over to her kite and climbed aboard. The other unicorns whinnied and cheered.

Cressida, thrilled her friend felt so much better, sang out, “Here I come!” as she skipped over to the remaining kite.

Chapter Nine

As soon as Cressida stepped onto her giant blue kite, the kite grinned and said, "Pleasure to meet you! My name is Kelly the Kite. We kites drew straws to see who would get to fly with the very first human girl to fly in the Blast. I was the lucky winner!"

"I can't wait," Cressida said. And then,

realizing she felt just a little bit nervous, she added, "I've never ridden a kite before."

"I promise to be extra careful so the ride isn't bumpy," Kelly said. "Just bend your knees a little, hold onto my reins, and you'll be fine." Cressida looked down and saw two sparkling blue strings. She grabbed them, bent her knees, and made sure her feet felt steady.

"Here we go!" Breeze called out. The aquamarine on her ribbon necklace shimmered. Blue, glittery light streamed from her horn. A gentle breeze riffled through Breeze's mane and tail before it blew toward the Meadow of Melodies. Soon Cressida heard "Twinkle, Twinkle, Little Star" playing once again. She smiled at the beauty of the wind chimes' music. Then, as more glittery light shot from Breeze's horn, the strongest gust of wind Cressida had ever felt swirled around Cressida and the unicorn princesses.

Cressida turned to Moon, who looked both excited and scared. "Just remember," Cressida said, "I don't think you'll fall off, but if you do, you're wearing a magic cape."

Kelly and all the other kites lifted off the ground. They formed a line in the air and began to fly in circles, each one higher than the last, as though they were climbing a spiral of wind. She looked down at the Windy Meadows, and then, in the distance, at the other unicorn princesses' domains: Sunbeam's purple Glitter Canyon, Flash's metallic Thunder Peaks, Bloom's green Enchanted Garden, Prism's rainbow-colored Valley of Light, Moon's dark Night Forest, and Firefly's glittery Shimmering Caves. Then she looked at each of the unicorns. All the sisters, including Moon, were grinning from ear to ear. No wonder Breeze and her sisters had been so excited to fly in the Blast.

When they reached the clouds, the kites—with Cressida and the unicorns aboard—flew upward through a long tube made of white fluff. At the end of the tube was an enormous floor made of clouds. They looked, Cressida thought, just like cotton balls. The kites landed, and

Kelly said, "Hop off! And congratulations on taking your first kite ride up to the magic clouds."

Cressida watched as the unicorns leaped off their kites and began jumping on the clouds and giggling. She dropped Kelly's reins and stepped onto the white fluffy floor. It felt soft, like a combination of a bouncy sponge and a cotton ball, under her feet. She jumped and found that she went high up into the air. It was like jumping on the biggest, bounciest mattress she could imagine. "This is so much fun!" she called out.

Breeze bounded over and jumped alongside Cressida. Sunbeam and Flash quickly joined in. And then Bloom, Prism, Moon, and Firefly rushed over, so Cressida and all the princess unicorns were jumping and laughing together.

"I'm so glad I decided to fly after all!" Moon sang out, jumping the highest of all the sisters.

"And I'm glad it was your decision to come with us, and not anyone else's!" Breeze said.

Just then, a voice chortled and then boomed, "The Blast Feast is ready!"

Cressida turned around and saw eight red dragons, all wearing white chef's hats and aprons, stirring gigantic silver vats. She had been so excited by jumping on the clouds that she hadn't even noticed the dragons before.

The same dragon that Cressida had seen carrying vats down to the palace kitchen stepped forward, smiled proudly, and announced, "We've cooked up stewed roinkleberries with creamed froyananas, roasted plums with froyanana sauce, avocado-froyanana soufflé, simmered corn and froyanana chowder, froyanana-oat-bragglenapple bars, froyanana-mango stir-fry, chocolate-eggplant pancakes with diced froyananas, and mushroom-froyanana tarts."

Cressida's stomach turned, and she grimaced at the thought of so many froyananas. Meanwhile, the princess unicorns looked ecstatic.

"Wow!" said Breeze, jumping in backward circles. "You outdid yourselves this year!"

"I can't wait!" Sunbeam exclaimed, dancing with excitement.

"This is the feast of my dreams! So many froyananas!" Bloom sang out.

The dragons laughed, and green flames and blue smoke rose from their nostrils as they emptied the contents of their vats into a row of gold and silver troughs. "Bon appétit!" the dragons called out. The unicorns rushed across the cloud floor and began to gobble down the food in the troughs.

"This stew is incredible!" gushed Moon between bites.

"And the soufflé is amazing," Prism added, licking her lips.

"It's the best chowder I've ever had," Bloom and Sunbeam said in unison.

Cressida smiled as she watched the unicorns eat. She was glad they were enjoying their feast. Just then, a dragon bounced over to her carrying a silver tray piled high with sliced roinkleberries. "Sunbeam

remembered how much you loved these," the dragon said. "All the other dishes have froyananas in them, and Bloom mentioned that, for some strange reason, you don't like those."

"Thank you!" Cressida said. She had first eaten roinkleberries on her first trip to the Rainbow Realm, when she'd visited the Glitter Canyon with Sunbeam, and she knew she loved them.

As Cressida ate the sweet fruit, she realized it was probably about time to go home and fly her own homemade kite up into the clouds above her backyard. She was eager to see Corey, even if she couldn't tell him about her adventures or how he and his book about bats had helped her get the bats off the giant kites. She hoped he still wanted to make a giant bat kite, and she wanted to help him do it.

"You look like you're thinking about going home," Breeze said, looking up from her trough.

"I've had such a wonderful time here," Cressida said, "and I loved the Blast. Thank you so very much for including me. But I do think it's time for me to go home. I'm looking forward to flying kites with my brother."

"You have kites in the human world?" Breeze asked, eyes widening.

"Yes," Cressida said. "In fact, I was making my very first homemade kite this morning when you called me. The only thing I had left to do was make the tail."

"Wow," Breeze said. "Have fun flying it."

Moon took a final bite of the food in her trough and trotted over to Cressida, still wearing her blue, sequined cape. "I heard you say you're about to leave," she said. "Thank you so much for lending me your magic cape. I know I should give it back to you, but," she said, blushing, "I was wondering if I could keep it to wear later on when we all fly back down to the ground."

"Of course," Cressida said, smiling. "I don't need it in the human world. I'm not really a superhero after all."

Then, Flash, Sunbeam, Bloom, Prism, and Firefly joined Cressida, Moon, and Breeze.

"Good bye!" Flash and Sunbeam said.

"Come again soon!" Prism and Bloom said.

"We'll invite you back in no time," Moon said, and Firefly nodded.

Cressida pulled the old-fashioned key with the crystal ball handle from her back pocket. "Take me home, please," she said. The clouds and sky began to spin around her, faster and faster, until they were a swirl of blue and white. Then, everything went pitch black—as dark as Moon had made the Windy Meadows—and Cressida felt the sensation of soaring through the air. She always liked that part of leaving the Rainbow Realm best, but today she especially liked it because it reminded her of flying Kelly the Kite up into the magic clouds.

Soon Cressida felt herself land on the soft forest floor. At first, the trees and sky spun in a blur of green, brown, and blue. Then, the woods slowed to a stop and she found herself sitting beneath the oak tree with the key still in her hands. She stood up, and as she pushed the key into her pocket, she felt something unfamiliar. She pulled it out to discover a long string of the same blue sequins that had been on her magic cape. Attached to the string, a note read,

Here's a magic tail for your kite.

Love, Breeze

Cressida smiled. And then she skipped back toward her house, ready to tie the sequin string to her unicorn kite and fly it in her backyard.

Unicorn Princesses

Moon's Dance

Chapter One

In the top tower of Spiral Palace, Ernest, a wizard-lizard, leafed through a dusty book entitled *Formal Wear for Feathered Friends.* As he turned the pages with his scaly fingers, a bird with messy red feathers and bright green eyes grinned with excitement and hopped from one foot to the other.

Ernest looked up from a page that read,

"Magic Spells for Beginners: Wingtips for Woodpeckers and Spats for Sparrows." He furrowed his green brow and cleared his throat. "Bernadette," he said, "let me make sure I'm getting this right. You want me to turn one of your head feathers into a ball gown?"

"Exactly," Bernadette said. "Last year, I wore an emerald green tuxedo to the Starlight Ball. It matched my eyes perfectly. But this year I want to try a ball gown. I have so many feathers on the top of my head," she continued, looking up at her thick, messy head plumage and grinning sheepishly, "that I was thinking I could spare one to make the perfect dress."

Ernest nodded and flipped to a page

with the words, "Advanced Spells: Turning Feathers and Plumes into Gowns," in large, gold letters across the top. He read for several seconds and asked, "You don't happen to know what a plume is, do you?"

"It's just a fancy word for a feather," Bernadette said, shrugging.

"Then I think I've found just the right spell," Ernest said.

"Fantastic!" Bernadette said, twirling on one talon while she kicked the other foot in the air. "I've been practicing my dance moves all week."

Ernest laughed. "Me too! And I've almost perfected the spell for my tuxedo." He blushed and added, "It just needs a few, um, tweaks." He straightened his pointy hat and pulled his wand from his cloak pocket. "Are you ready for your ball gown?"

"Absolutely!" Bernadette said.

Ernest lifted his wand, pointed it at an unruly feather on Bernadette's head, and chanted, "Feathery Fancily Pleathery Plown! Turn this Ballroom into a Crown!" He stared expectantly at Bernadette. But instead of a gown appearing, thunder rumbled and a giant bolt of gold lightning tore across the sky.

"Oh dear," Ernest said, grimacing. "What did I do wrong this time?"

Bernadette peered over at the open page in Ernest's book. "Well," she said, pointing with her talon, "I'm pretty sure you read this line incorrectly."

"Oh dear! I sure did," Ernest said. "Let me try one more time." He studied the spell, mouthing the words silently. Then he looked again at Bernadette, pointed his wand at the same feather, and chanted, "Feathery Fancily Pleathery Plown! Turn this Small Plume into a Gown!"

Red light swirled around Bernadette, and suddenly she was wearing a scarlet ball gown with a sequined top and a gauzy skirt. "I love it!" Bernadette cried as she shimmied and sashayed across the room. "It's perfect for dancing. Thank you, Ernest!" And then she hopped out the door and twirled down the hall.

Chapter Two

On a rainy Wednesday afternoon, Cressida Jenkins stood in the middle of her bedroom wearing a black leotard, pink tights, pink ballet slippers, and a turquoise tutu. She glanced at her bedroom door to triple check it was closed and locked. She didn't want Corey, her older brother, to walk in and see her practicing for her dance recital that weekend. If he did, he would never stop making fun of her tutu or the way she danced.

Cressida took a deep breath. She pressed the play button on her music player. And then, as she counted in her head, she leaped, spun, and twirled across her unicorn rug. At the end of her dance routine, as she prepared to curtsy, she heard a high, tinkling noise. At first she thought it was a part of the song she didn't remember. And then she realized the sound was coming from her bedside table drawer.

Cressida's heart skipped a beat and her eyes widened. She turned off her music player and bounded over to her bedside table. She opened the drawer and pulled

out an old-fashioned key with a crystal-ball handle that glowed bright pink. Cressida beamed with excitement. Her friends, the unicorn princesses, had given her the key so she could visit them in their secret world, the Rainbow Realm, any time: all she had to do was push the key into a hole in the base of a giant oak tree in the woods behind her house, and she would be magically transported to the unicorns' home, Spiral Palace. When the unicorns wanted to invite Cressida to join them for a special occasion, they made the key's handle turn bright pink—just the way it was glowing right then!

As quickly as she could, Cressida peeled off her leotard, tights, slippers, and tutu—the tights were too scratchy to wear all afternoon, and she didn't want to worry about tearing her tutu, which she would need for her recital, while she rode unicorns in the Rainbow Realm. She put on rainbow-striped leggings, a black T-shirt covered in gold stars, a green zip-up sweatshirt with a picture of a raccoon on the back, and silver unicorn sneakers. The sneakers were her favorite shoes: not only did they have pictures of unicorns on them, but they also had pink lights that blinked whenever she jumped, walked, or ran.

Cressida slipped the magic key into her sweatshirt pocket and skipped out of her room and down the hall toward the back door. She picked up the first umbrella she saw—an old black-and-yellow-striped one—and called out to her mother, "I'm going for a quick walk in the woods."

"Don't you want to wait until it stops raining?" her mother asked from the living room.

"I've got an umbrella," Cressida said. "And besides, I'm only going outside for a few minutes." Fortunately, time in the human world froze while Cressida was in the Rainbow Realm, meaning that even if she spent hours with the unicorns, her mother would think she had been gone only fifteen minutes.

"I suppose a little rain never hurt any-one," her mother said. "Have fun!"

Cressida hopped out the door, opened the umbrella, jogged across her soggy backyard, and found the trail that led through the woods to the oak tree with the magic keyhole. She couldn't wait to see her unicorn friends: yellow Princess Sunbeam, silver Princess Flash, green Princess Bloom, purple Princess Prism, blue Princess Breeze, black Princess Moon, and orange Princess Firefly.

When she got to the oak tree, she leaned her umbrella against the trunk so it would be waiting for her when she returned to the human world. She smiled for a moment at the feeling of the rain on her face and hands. And then she kneeled, pulled the key from her sweatshirt pocket, and pushed it into the tiny hole in the tree's base. The forest began to spin, until all she could see was a blur of blue, green, and brown. Then the forest turned pitch black, and Cressida felt as though she were tumbling through space. After several seconds, she landed on something soft.

At first, all Cressida could see was a swirl of silver, white, pink, and purple. But when the room stopped spinning, she found herself sitting on a pink velvet couch. Glittering chandeliers hung from the ceiling. Pink and purple curtains fluttered in the air. Cressida smiled. She knew exactly where she was—in the front hall of Spiral Palace, the unicorn princesses' sparkling white, horn-shaped home.

Chapter Three

Across the room, a raccoon with lime-green stripes played a harp with his front paws and a drum with his tail as all seven unicorn princesses—wearing capes and glittering crowns that matched their magic gemstone necklaces—danced. Sunbeam twirled in a yellow sapphire crown and a gold cape dotted with sun-shaped sequins. Flash, wearing a diamond crown and a gauzy silver cape decorated with copper lightning bolts, did perfect pirouettes. Bloom, in an emerald crown and a mint-green cape with a glittery flower design, sashayed and pranced. Prism wore an amethyst crown and a purple taffeta cape with rainbow trim as she leaped and spun. Breeze, in an aquamarine crown and a blue cape embroidered with white swirls, and Firefly, in a citrine tiara and a shiny orange cape, swayed together to the beat. Moon, in an opal crown and a black silk cape with bronze stars, leaped and spun in circles as she swished her tail.

For a few seconds, Cressida smiled as she watched her friends. Then, she stood up

and sang out, “Hello there!” as she skipped toward them.

“My human girl is back!” Sunbeam called out, jumping straight up into the air and clicking her hooves together three times before she landed with a clatter on the marble floor.

“Welcome!” Flash said, rearing up.

“We’re so happy to see you!” Bloom and Prism said as they shimmied toward Cressida.

“We’re excited you could come,” Breeze and Firefly said, grinning.

“Cressida! I’m thrilled you’re here!” Moon exclaimed, racing over to Cressida and trotting in circles around her. “We were just practicing our dance moves for the Starlight Ball this afternoon. How did we look?"

"Amazing," Cressida said. She couldn't wait to hear more about the Starlight Ball. And she thought it was neat that, without even knowing it, she and the unicorns had been dancing that afternoon at exactly the same time.

Moon and her sisters blushed. "Well, thank you," Moon said, flicking strands of her silky black mane out of her eyes. The opals on her golden-yellow ribbon necklace and her crown twinkled. She turned to the raccoon, who had stopped playing music. "Cressida, this is Ringo. He and the other raccoons in my domain, the Night Forest, play traditional unicorn music every year for the ball. And this year, for the first time, the raccoons might even play some new music they wrote themselves."

"It's wonderful to meet you," Cressida said. "I love your music."

"Why, thank you," Ringo said, tucking the harp under his arm and wrapping his long, striped tail around the drum. "I'm sorry to dash off, but I have to head back to the Night Forest for a practice session with the other raccoons." He waved and scurried away carrying his instruments.

"I have a question for you," Moon said, twirling on her shiny black hooves. "How would you like to be the first human girl to attend the Starlight Ball? It's a spectacular dance I host every year in the Night Forest's very own ballroom."

"That sounds wonderful," Cressida said, jumping with excitement. "I've always wanted to go to a ball!"

"You've never been to a ball?" Flash and Sunbeam asked, looking surprised.

Cressida shook her head.

"Not even one?" asked Firefly.

"Not even one!" Cressida said, amused.

"But if you've never been to a ball, when do you wear your crown?" Bloom blurted out.

Cressida giggled. "I don't have a crown," she said.

"You don't have a crown?" Flash,

Sunbeam, and Bloom said at once, eyes wide.

"Nope!" Cressida said, laughing even harder.

"The human world is such a strange place," Prism said, winking at Cressida.

"Now that I know you've never been to a ball, I'm even more excited you're here for the Starlight Ball," Moon gushed. "How would you like to come with me to help finish decorating the ballroom? Breeze and Firefly said they'd meet us there a little before the ball to help, too. If we go soon, we might even have time to listen to the raccoons' final practice session."

"I'd love that," Cressida said.

Just then, Ernest skipped into the room

wearing a glittery silver tuxedo, matching wingtips, and a sequined purple top hat.

"I've been practicing this tuxedo spell all week," Ernest announced with a wide grin. "How do I look?"

He spun around, and as he turned, Cressida noticed that instead of tails on

the back of Ernest's tuxedo coat, there hung two long, dark-green leaves.

Sunbeam, Bloom, and Prism looked at each other and smiled.

"I love your hat, but your tuxedo . . ." Flash began.

"You look ready to dance, except . . ." Moon started.

"What's wrong?" Ernest asked, his grin folding into a worried frown. "You don't like my tuxedo?"

"Your tuxedo looks great," Firefly said. "It's just that, well, I think something might have gone wrong with the back of your jacket."

Ernest blushed and grimaced. "Oh dear," he said. "Did I say 'mail' instead of 'tail' again? There are already stacks and stacks of envelopes all over my room."

"I think," Cressida said, recognizing the leaves from a vegetable dish her father often made for dinner, "you might have said 'kale.' "

"Oh dear!" Ernest said. "I'm so embarrassed."

"It's okay," Moon said. "You still have time to work on your tuxedo spell before the Starlight Ball. And if you can't get it right, there's nothing wrong with wearing leafy green vegetables on your coat."

"The worst-case scenario is you'll have an emergency snack on your jacket," Bloom added, winking at Ernest.

Ernest laughed. "I guess I'd better keep

practicing," he said. "But first, I want to make a ball gown for Cressida! I already made one without a glitch—well, almost without a glitch—for another friend this morning."

"Uh oh," Moon whispered to Cressida. "The next thing you know, you'll be wearing a spinach tutu!"

"I heard that!" Ernest said.

"I'd love a ball gown," Cressida said, jumping with excitement. "Do you think there's any chance you could make one with pockets? I like to have somewhere to put things."

"Of course!" Ernest said. He cleared his throat. He pulled his wand out from under his top hat. And he waved it at Cressida as he chanted, "Formally Normally Dancily Dockets! Make a Small Town with Two Big Rockets!"

Suddenly, at Cressida's feet there appeared a bustling miniature town, complete with roads, houses, train tracks, a hospital, a movie theater, and a school. In the center, right next to the school, were two rockets with bright red noses pointed toward the sky. Four tiny astronauts pushed a ladder against the side of one of the rockets, just below the door, and began to climb up. When Cressida bent over to examine the rockets more closely, she noticed little cars, trucks, and buses driving over the toes of her unicorn sneakers.

"Oh dear!" Ernest said. "Hold on! I can

do it right this time!" He held up his wand and chanted, "Snickety Snackety Snippety Snockets! Away with the Small Town and Two Large Rockets! Next Make a Ball Gown with Two Big Pockets!"

A bright pink light swirled around Cressida. She blinked and shut her eyes.

When she opened them, she looked down to see she was wearing a ball gown with a gold and pink sequined top and a gauzy pink skirt covered in gold glitter. Best of all, the gown had two enormous pink pockets. Cressida beamed. "I love it!" she said, and she plunged her hands into the pockets. Inside one, she felt her magic key. She smiled, glad to have it with her. Then, she spun and twirled in her new dress.

"What do you think?" Cressida asked.

"What a fabulous gown!" Moon exclaimed. "You look ready to go to a ball!"

"I knew I could do it!" Ernest said. "And now I'd better go work on a new tuxedo jacket."

"Before you go," Moon said, "I wonder if I could ask you for one more magical favor."

"Of course," Ernest said. "Anything at all."

Moon leaned over and whispered in Ernest's ear. He nodded as she spoke.

"Excellent idea," Ernest said. "I should have thought of that myself."

"Do you want to go check in one of your spell books before you try it?" Moon asked. "We most certainly don't mind waiting."

"No need," Ernest said. "I've got just the spell."

"But I really do think—" Moon began.

Before she could say another word, Ernest lifted his wand and chanted, "Darkily

Markily Mightily Sight! Please Make Cressida Glasses for Night!"

Wind swirled around Cressida. Suddenly, in her right hand, she held a pair of glasses with pink frames dotted with opals that matched Moon's gemstone.

For a moment, Ernest stared at the glasses. He blinked as his mouth hung open. And then he sang out, "I did it! I did it! I did it on the first try! That's never happened before!"

Cressida giggled and clapped. The unicorn princesses cheered. Ernest bowed several times. And then he tap-danced across the room and down the hall, singing, "I did it! And now to get this kale off my tuxedo!"

Chapter Four

After Ernest disappeared down the hall, dancing and singing, Cressida looked again at her new glasses. "Should I put these on now?" she asked.

"Not yet," Moon said. "But I'm pretty sure you'll need them once we get to the Night Forest."

Cressida nodded and slid the glasses into her empty pocket. When she looked up, she noticed that Breeze and Firefly were frowning, whispering, and glancing at Moon.

"Is something wrong?" Moon asked. "If you don't have time to meet Cressida and me at the ballroom to help finish decorating, I completely understand."

"It's not that," Breeze said, looking worried.

"It's just that—" Firefly began. She sighed, furrowed her brow, and continued, "We heard you mention that Ringo and the other raccoons might play their new music at the ball."

"And we wanted to ask if we could stick to the traditional unicorn music," Breeze said.

"Why?" Moon asked, looking surprised.

"We don't know how to dance to the new music," Breeze explained. "And the one time I tried, I tripped and fell over."

Moon giggled. "That's because at the same time you were dancing you were also blindfolded and trying to break a piñata with your horn."

Breeze blushed. "Well, I guess that's true," she said. "But that doesn't change the fact that I don't know how to dance to it. And I'm afraid I'll look silly and feel awkward if I try again. The ball is supposed to be fun, and the new music will completely ruin it."

Firefly nodded. "I already have enough trouble dancing to the traditional unicorn music, and whenever I hear the new music, I freeze up," she said. "It will spoil everything."

Moon took a deep breath. "I don't know how to dance to the raccoons' new music either," she said, "but I think it would be fun to learn how. And it would make the raccoons so happy to get to play the songs they've written." She smiled hopefully at her sisters.

Breeze and Firefly looked at each other and whispered. Then they both shook their heads. "If the raccoons play the new music, we might have to leave early," Firefly said.

"Or we might not come at all," Breeze said.

"It will ruin the ball," they said at the same time.

"I just thought it might be fun to try something new," Moon said. Her hopeful smile bent into a disappointed frown. She looked like she might start crying.

Cressida put her arm around Moon's neck. She knew exactly how Moon felt: often, it was exciting to listen to new music or eat new food or read a new kind of book. But she also understood Breeze and Firefly's perspective: feeling uncomfortable was pretty miserable, especially at a dance.

"Maybe you need a little bit of time to think about what to do," Cressida said to Moon.

"Yes," Moon said, brightening. "I need some time to think about it." She closed her eyes and took a deep breath. Then she smiled, turned to Cressida, and asked, "Are you ready to help prepare for your very first ball?"

"Absolutely," Cressida said. Moon kneeled and Cressida climbed onto her back.

"We'll still plan on meeting you at the Night Forest ballroom an hour before the ball starts," Breeze said.

Firefly nodded. "Just please tell the

raccoons to stick to the traditional music," she added.

"I'll think about it," Moon said. "See you soon!" Then, with Cressida on her back, she galloped across the front hall of Spiral Palace and out the door.

As Cressida held onto Moon's silky black mane, the unicorn hopped along the clear stones that led away from the palace and into the surrounding forest. For a few seconds, Cressida turned and gazed back at Spiral Palace. She grinned as she spied a flash of silver and a sparkle of purple through the window of the palace's top tower. She bet Ernest was up there, perfecting his tuxedo spell.

"Thanks for suggesting I take a little more time to make a decision about the music," Moon said. "I think it would be so much fun to learn to dance to the raccoons' new music. The traditional unicorn music is fine, but, to be honest, I get bored dancing to the same songs over and over again."

"I love learning to dance to new music, too," Cressida said. One of her favorite things about her ballet class was that she learned to dance to music she had never heard before.

"Well," said Moon, taking a deep breath, "maybe if we get to the Night Forest in time to listen in on the raccoons' final practice session, you can let me know if you think it's possible to dance to their new music. And in the meantime, I can't wait to show you the Night Forest!"

Chapter Five

With Cressida on her back, Moon turned right on a narrow path that wove through a grove of cherry and maple trees, and then galloped along a thick hedge covered in thorny vines with bright yellow, crescent-shaped flowers. She stopped in front of a hole in the hedge that was just a few inches taller than the tip of her horn. "This is the entrance to the Night Forest," she said. "Close your eyes!"

Cressida shut her eyes as Moon took several steps forward. Cressida heard crickets chirping and bull frogs croaking. Owls called out, "Hoo! Hoo!" In the distance, a wolf howled.

"Now you can look!" Moon said. Cressida opened her eyes. Above her, the moon, like a pale banana, hung amid more tiny silver stars than she had ever seen. In the light of the moon and stars, she could make out the shapes of a pond, a meadow, and what looked like it might be the edge of a dark forest. Even though she could see about as well as she could in her bedroom with her unicorn nightlight switched on, she had to admit she wished she had a flashlight.

"I can't see very well," Cressida said, gripping Moon's mane more tightly.

"I had a feeling humans can't see in the dark as well as unicorns," Moon said. "Try putting on the glasses Ernest made for you."

Cressida slid her hand into her pocket, pulled out her glasses, and put them on. Now she could see a pond with shimmering black water. Giant blue frogs with glowing orange eyes perched on the lily pads and croaked, their balloon throats bulging. On one side of the pond, a family of opossums lumbered through a meadow of thick, high grass. On the other side was a forest thick

with trees and vines. White and silver owls perched in the tree branches, their glowing yellow eyes winking at Cressida.

"Wow!" Cressida said. "The Night Forest is beautiful."

"I thought you'd like it," Moon said. "Can you see well enough to walk?"

"Yes," Cressida said. "These glasses are perfect. Thank you for thinking of them."

"No problem," Moon said, kneeling down as Cressida slid off her back. "Come this way."

Cressida and Moon followed a path carpeted in spongy green moss into the forest. Soon the mossy trail disappeared, and thick vines, tree roots, and rocks covered the forest floor. It was difficult not to stumble or trip, especially while wearing a ball gown.

Soon Cressida and Moon stepped into a grove of gnarled cedar trees growing among vines and roots so thick and knotted Cressida wasn't sure if she could keep walking without falling over. Moon paused, turned to Cressida, and smiled excitedly. "Want to see my favorite part of the Night Forest?" she asked.

"Absolutely," Cressida said. Then she looked up from the forest floor to notice hundreds and hundreds of gray stars, each about the size of a book, dangling from the tree branches.

"Do you mind if I make it so dark your special glasses won't work?" Moon asked.

"No problem," Cressida said. She wasn't usually afraid of the dark.

"I can't wait to show you Midnight Stars," Moon said. "Their magic only works when it's pitch black."

Moon pointed her horn toward the sky. The opal on her ribbon necklace twinkled. Sparkling light poured from her horn. Suddenly, it was so dark that Cressida couldn't even see her hands when she held them in front of her face. Though she wasn't afraid, she had to admit she felt a little nervous. She reached for Moon's back. When her fingers touched her friend's soft coat, she took a deep breath.

Just then, the stars on the trees began to glow. At first, their light was faint. But after a few seconds, they brightened and began to change color: from white to yellow to orange and, finally, to a vibrant red. Soon, the forest glowed a spectacular shade of scarlet.

"Wow!" Cressida said. "The Midnight Stars are beautiful."

"I thought you'd like them," said Moon. "And that's not all they can do." She cleared her throat and called out, "Midnight Stars, please take us to the raccoons!"

The stars began to wiggle, jiggle, and swing on the branches. Then they lifted off the trees, swirled in circles above Cressida and Moon's heads, and dropped to the forest floor in the shape of a long, glowing trail. "This way we don't have to walk on all those roots and vines," Moon said as she stepped onto the pathway of stars. They sparkled like rubies as her hooves touched them.

Cressida stepped onto the glowing pathway, and the stars shimmered. She took another step, and noticed that the stars

were quite smooth. They weren't slippery, like ice, but they were perfect for spinning and twirling, even in sneakers. Cressida turned and jumped as she walked, giggling.

Moon watched her and laughed, and then they both sashayed forward.

Soon Cressida and Moon were leaping and twirling together along a path of stars that led through groves of towering pine trees, beds of giant ferns, clusters of flowering vines, and marshes full of reeds and pussy willows. Then the trail of stars made a sharp right and ended in a sea of darkness that Cressida guessed was a meadow, though with all the stars' red light behind her, she couldn't see well enough to be sure.

"We'd better tidy up the Midnight Stars

before we go see the raccoons," Moon said. She shrugged and added, "Though I have to admit that I love it when it's pitch black." She pointed her horn to the sky. Her opal shimmered, and sparkling light poured from her horn. The Night Forest grew lighter, and immediately the stars began to wiggle and jiggle. Then they lifted into the air and flew in circles as they turned from bright red to orange to yellow to white and, finally, to a lightless gray. Then, like a school of fish, they bolted back into the woods.

"Thanks so much for showing me the Midnight Stars," Cressida said.

"My pleasure," Moon said. "Are you

ready to listen to the raccoons' practice session?"

"Yes," Cressida said. She turned to see that they were, in fact, standing in front of a meadow. And among the grass and wild-flowers were the biggest oak trees Cressida had ever seen—they were much bigger than the one with the magic keyhole in the woods behind her house!

As Cressida and Moon walked into the meadow, Cressida noticed that spiral stair-cases, made of thousands of twigs fastened together with pine needles, wound around the trees and ended at oval-shaped doors midway up the trunks.

Moon paused in front of the biggest tree

and stepped onto the stairs. "The raccoons built these staircases just for me," Moon said. "Otherwise, it's not really possible to climb a tree if you have hooves. Want to come up?"

"Yes, please!" Cressida said, grinning. She had always, ever since she was a little girl, wanted to visit a raccoon in a hollow tree. Now she was going to get to do just that! She followed Moon up the stairs, holding up her ball gown.

At the top, with Cressida right behind her, Moon knocked on the door with her hoof. "Hello?" she called out. "It's me, Princess Moon."

"Princess Moon! Come on in," said a

voice from inside the tree. "Did you bring Cressida?"

"I sure did!" Moon said, nudging the door open with her nose. Then, she and Cressida walked inside.

The first thing Cressida noticed inside the hollow tree was that nearly everywhere she looked—hanging on the walls, lined up on shelves, even stacked on the floor—were musical instruments. Some looked like instruments she recognized from the human world: there were guitars, banjos, violins, flutes, clarinets, trumpets, trombones, saxophones, drums, xylophones, and triangles. But there were also instruments Cressida had never seen before, with curly pipes, strings at odd angles, many-sided drums, and spiraling keyboards.

In the center of the room four raccoons, each with lime-green stripes and mask, sat in a circle holding their instruments.

"Cressida, these are my good friends," Moon said, nodding toward the raccoons. "You've already met Ringo." He smiled and waved at Cressida. "And here are Renee, Roland, and Rita. In addition to playing traditional unicorn music on harps and drums, the Night Forest raccoons invent and build new instruments and write their own songs."

"Wow!" Cressida said. "It's wonderful to meet you. Thank you for letting me visit your hollow tree."

"The pleasure is ours," Ringo said.

"We've always wanted to meet a human girl," Renee explained, twitching her whiskers.

"We've heard the human world has wonderful music," Roland said. "I've wanted to visit, but I have a feeling someone might think a green raccoon listening to music was just a little odd."

Cressida giggled. "Probably," she said. "But you could all come listen to music with me in my room anytime! I wouldn't think that was odd at all."

"That would be fantastic!" Ringo said, grinning.

Rita stared for several seconds at Cressida's face. "Those are such wonderful glasses," she said. "You almost look like one of us!"

"Thank you," Cressida said. "They help me see in the dark."

"You can't see in the dark?" Renee and Roland said at once.

"I can't even imagine what that would be like," Rita said.

"Is it strange to need light to see?" Ringo asked.

"It's not strange to me," Cressida said, shrugging and smiling.

The raccoons nodded, fascinated.

Then Ringo said, "We were just practicing some new music we've been writing together. We're hoping Moon will let us play it at the ball. Would you like to hear it?"

"Absolutely!" Cressida said. "But first, will you tell me the names of your instruments?"

Ringo grinned. "This one," he said, nodding to an instrument that looked like a harp with four flutes poking out from the bottom and a drum on top, "is a flarpophone." He pointed to Renee's instrument, which looked like a large banjo with four blue keyboards wrapped around its body. "This is a quadruple-duple-banjinano." He laid a paw on Roland's instrument, which looked like five trumpets welded to the top of an accordion. "This is a trumpledumpledordion." He pointed to Rita's instrument, which looked like eight long, thin, curly saxophones arranged in a circle. It reminded

Cressida of an octopus. "And we just built this one today," Ringo said. "We're calling it an octogoloctohorn."

"Amazing!" Cressida said. "If you'd like to play your new music now, I'd love to hear it."

"Me too," Moon said.

Ringo, Rita, Roland, and Renee smiled and nodded at each other. Ringo tapped the side of his flarpophone as he counted, "One and a two and a one, two, three, four." The raccoons began to play, blowing into pipes and mouthpieces, strumming strings, crawling with their fingers up and down keyboards, and thumping on drums with their tails. The music sounded like a combination of the jazz her father listened to, the rock and roll her mother liked, and the show tunes her friends Daphne, Eleanor, and Gillian loved. The more she listened, the more she couldn't keep her toes from tapping. Soon her body was swaying, her feet were stepping, and her arms were waving.

She glanced over at Moon, who was swaying with the beat and furrowing her brow. "I really want to dance," she whispered, "but to be honest, I'm not sure how."

"Try doing this," Cressida said, stepping back and forth and waving her arms.

Moon took a step and then stopped. Her face looked uncertain.

"You can do it," Cressida whispered gently, twirling and kicking to the beat.

Moon slowly took another step and tried to swish her tail. And then she froze. "Maybe Breeze and Firefly are right and we should stick with the traditional unicorn music," Moon said, her face falling. "I want to dance to the new music. I really do. But I feel so worried about looking silly that I can't. Though I sure would hate to disappoint the raccoons by telling them not to play their new songs."

Cressida paused and thought about how to help her friend. She decided that the raccoons' new music wasn't the kind of music that you danced to by learning certain steps and sequences of dance moves, the way she did in her ballet class. Instead, it was the kind of music you danced to by making up your own ways of moving. "I don't think there's a right way or a wrong way to dance to this music," Cressida said. "Try closing your eyes and letting your body move in whatever way it wants to."

"But what if I look ridiculous?" Moon asked.

"Then we'll look ridiculous together," Cressida said, winking at Moon.

Moon smiled, even though she still looked nervous. She closed her eyes. For a few seconds she simply stepped back and forth. But soon, keeping her eyes tightly shut, she began to twirl, rear up, click her hooves together, and jump. For a moment, Cressida watched her friend. And then she closed her eyes too and began to spin and jump with the music. After a while, Cressida opened her eyes to discover Moon's eyes were open, too. The two looked at each other and began to dance together: twirling at the same time, nodding their heads to the beat, skipping and prancing around the inside of the hollow tree.

When the raccoons stopped playing their music, Moon and Cressida, both out of breath, burst out laughing.

"That was the most fun I've ever had dancing!" Moon said.

"Me too," Cressida said.

"Thank you!" the raccoons said, smiling proudly. Then all four stood up and took a bow.

Ringo cleared his throat. "Princess Moon, there is something we wanted to ask," he began. "Have you decided whether we can play our new music at the ball?"

"I'm still thinking about it," Moon said. "Breeze and Firefly really want us to stick to the traditional unicorn songs because they're worried they won't know how to dance to the new music." Moon smiled at Cressida. "But it's pretty clear there are all kinds of ways to dance to it."

Ringo, Rita, Roland, and Renee exchanged hopeful glances.

"I just need a little more time to make a decision," Moon said.

Ringo nodded. "Would you like us to play another new song?" he asked. "We could play a really fast one that's even better for dancing."

"Oh, thank you so much for offering," Moon said. "I'd love to keep dancing, but I think Cressida and I had better go finish decorating the ballroom. There are more balloons and more strings of glow-in-the-dark rainbows I want to put up. And Breeze and Firefly are going to meet us there soon to help out."

Cressida nodded. She wanted to stay and dance in the hollow tree for at least another hour or two, but she also felt excited to see the ballroom. "Thank you so very much for introducing me to your instruments and playing your new music for me," she said.

"Our pleasure!" Ringo, Roland, Rita, and Renee all said at once.

"See you at the Starlight Ball," Moon said.

And with that, Cressida followed Moon out the door and down the steps that spiraled around the tree trunk to the ground.

Chapter Six

"I can't wait to show you the ballroom," Moon said as she stepped off the spiral staircase and into the grassy meadow. "The raccoons, wolves, owls, opossums, frogs, and I all designed and built it together out of rocks, tree branches, twigs, and pine cones."

Cressida followed Moon past more oak trees and through a jungle of tall, white diamond-shaped flowers. "The ballroom is just around this corner," Moon said as the path jutted sharply to the left.

As soon as they turned, Moon stopped short. "Oh no," she gasped.

"What's wrong?" Cressida asked, looking all around for the ballroom. All she could see was a clearing with a large, muddy circle littered with rocks.

"Something happened to the ballroom," Moon said, dipping a hoof in the mud and frowning.

"It was here?" Cressida asked, trying to imagine how a ballroom—even one made of rocks, tree branches, twigs, and pine cones—could just suddenly disappear.

"Yes," Moon said, her voice wavering.

"I bet it's another of Ernest's magical mishaps. He means well, but he really is pretty terrible at magic." A tear slid down Moon's cheek. "Well, I guess we'll have to cancel the ball. We certainly can't dance in this mud."

"I'm so sorry the ballroom is gone," Cressida said, putting her arm around Moon. "But let's see if we can think of a way to still have the ball."

More tears slid down Moon's cheeks. "It took us months and months to build the ballroom," she said, her voice shaking. "I don't think we could possibly make another one in the next hour or two. I'm sure we'll have to cancel it."

"I'm not quite ready to give up," Cressida

said, smiling sympathetically at Moon. "I would be pretty disappointed not to get to go to my very first ball."

As Cressida tried to think of a way to save the Starlight Ball, she gazed out again at the circle of rocks and mud. And then she noticed something shiny right in the middle of where the ballroom had once been.

"What's that?" she asked, pointing to the shiny thing.

"I'm not sure," Moon said, sniffling. "Why don't we go see?"

Cressida pulled up the skirt of her ball gown as she walked toward the center of the circle, but she still managed to splatter mud all over her dress and her unicorn sneakers. She didn't mind. Life wouldn't be much fun if she spent all her time trying not to get dirty.

"I just polished my hooves this morning to get ready for the ball, and now they're getting all muddy," Moon said. "I guess it probably doesn't matter now."

In the center of the muddy, rocky circle where the ballroom had once been, Cressida crouched down to discover the shiny thing she and Moon had spotted: a crown made of thin gold wires, meant to look like vines, that twisted around bright pink, star-shaped sapphires. The sapphires, Cressida noticed, were exactly the same shade of pink as her ball gown. "It's beautiful," she said.

"It's gorgeous," Moon agreed, though her voice sounded sad. Then, with one of her muddy black hooves, she tried to move the crown. It wouldn't budge. Next, she tried to pick it up with her mouth. It still wouldn't move. "That's weird," Moon said. "Maybe it's stuck to a rock. Do you want to try?"

"Sure," Cressida said. She reached out and put her hands on the crown and pulled up, expecting she wouldn't be able to lift it. But to her surprise, it came right off the ground. As she held it in her hands, the crown began to glow and hum.

Moon gasped. "How on earth did you do that?" she asked.

"I don't know," Cressida said, feeling puzzled. "I just picked it up."

Moon tilted her head to the side. "How strange," she said. "Why don't you try putting it on?"

Cressida grinned and put the crown on her head. It felt light and comfortable, as though it belonged to her. For a moment, the humming noise got louder, and then a magic wand, made of a long, gold vine with a pink, star-shaped sapphire at the end, appeared in Cressida's hand.

"Wow!" Moon said, looking at

the crown and the wand. "Now you look like Princess Cressida. And not just Princess Cressida, but Magic Princess Cressida."

"You don't think this wand really is magic, do you?" Cressida asked, turning the wand over in her hand.

"It might be," Moon said, brightening. "Try waving it and see what happens."

"Okay," Cressida said, shrugging. She looked at a brown rock by her feet and waved her wand at it. She didn't expect anything to happen, but to her amazement, the star-shaped sapphire at the end sparkled, and light poured out. Then the rock disappeared and in its place grew a small, pink vine. Cressida giggled with delight and waved the wand at the vine again, this time holding the pink sapphire above the vine and lifting upward. The vine grew!

"I have magic powers!" Cressida sang out, jumping so that even more mud splattered all over her dress, her shoes, and Moon. Her unicorn friend smiled, but Cressida noticed her eyes looked even sadder and more disappointed than before.

"I'm so glad you have a new crown and a magic wand," Moon said, "but I have to confess I was hoping your special magic power would be to make a new ballroom appear."

Cressida put her arms around Moon and gave her a hug. "That would have been wonderful," Cressida agreed. And then, suddenly, she had an idea. "I think my new magic power might be the next best thing. I have a plan for how to build a new ballroom."

"Really?" Moon said, looking doubtful. "In just an hour?"

"Yes," Cressida said, looking at the pink vine for several seconds. "But we'll need some help from Breeze and Firefly."

"Well then, we're in luck," Moon said, smiling hopefully. "Look behind you."

Cressida turned around to see Breeze and Firefly galloping toward them.

Chapter Seven

For several seconds, Breeze and Firefly stared at the circle of rocks and mud. Then Breeze asked, "Where's the ballroom?"

"What happened?" Firefly asked.

Moon told Breeze and Firefly the story of how they had come to finish decorating the ballroom, only to find a giant circle of mud and rocks. "But look what Cressida found in the middle of all the mud," Moon said, pointing her horn toward Cressida.

Breeze and Firefly noticed Cressida's crown and wand and grinned.

"I call her Magic Princess Cressida," Moon said. "Especially because she says she has a plan to save the Starlight Ball."

"If anyone can save the Starlight Ball, it's Magic Princess Cressida," Breeze said.

"Definitely," Firefly added.

Cressida blushed. "It's true that I have an idea," she said. "But I'll need your help."

"Of course," Breeze and Firefly said at once.

But then Breeze paused and looked at Moon. "Did you make a decision about the music?" she asked.

Moon grinned. "Yes," she said. "Cressida and I visited the raccoons during their practice session, and we had an amazing time dancing to their new music. It turns out it's even easier to dance to than the traditional unicorn music! I've decided that if Cressida can find a way to save the ball, I'm going to ask them to only play their new music. And then Cressida and I will teach everyone to dance to it."

Cressida felt surprised, but she had to admit she wasn't disappointed. The most fun she had ever had dancing had been in the hollow tree.

Firefly frowned.

Breeze sighed and shook her head. "Please, Moon," she said. "Let's not risk ruining the ball. Let's ask the raccoons to stick to the traditional music."

Firefly nodded. "I've been practicing my traditional unicorn dances all week. I don't want to spend the entire ball standing by the wall watching everyone else dance or feeling awkward and silly on the dance floor."

"But—" Moon began. She looked down at her hooves. "I really think we could all learn to dance to the new music together. It will be fun."

Breeze sighed and shook her head. "I don't really feel like helping to build a new ballroom knowing that I probably won't even want to stay at the ball."

"Me neither," Firefly said, frowning.

Suddenly, Moon, Breeze, and Firefly all looked like they might start crying.

Cressida took a deep breath. "I have an idea," she said. "I can completely understand that Breeze and Firefly want to have a great time at the ball, and that they're worried the wrong music will ruin it. And I can also see why Moon wants the raccoons to play the new music. She and I had a fantastic time dancing to it together just a few minutes ago." The unicorns all nodded. "So," Cressida continued, "why don't we compromise?"

"What does 'compromise' mean?" Firefly asked.

"Is that the name of the dance you made up to the new music?" Breeze asked, turning up her nose.

Cressida laughed. "'Compromise' means we make an agreement with each other where we all get some of the things we want, but not everything," she explained. "Instead of one of you getting your way, we could come up with a solution that takes all of you into consideration. My brother and I have to compromise all the time when we don't agree on what games we want to play."

"That sounds good," Moon said.

"Let's try it," Firefly said.

Breeze nodded.

"How about," Cressida said, "we ask the raccoons to alternate between old songs and new songs at the ball? That way, if there's a song one of you doesn't want to dance to, it won't be so bad because you know you'll like the next one."

Moon thought for a few seconds and said, "I'd be willing to do that."

Firefly shrugged and nodded. "I'd agree to that."

Breeze paused and sighed. "I guess that would be okay," she finally said, still sounding unsure. "But I'm still worried I'll have a miserable time. I'm not very good at dancing to the traditional unicorn music, and I've been doing that my whole life. I'd hate to have to sit out for half the ball if I just can't learn to dance to the new music."

Just as Cressida tried to think of another suggestion, Moon said, "I have an idea for another compromise." She turned to Breeze. "How about if you agree to try your hardest to dance to the new music?

And in exchange, I'll promise that if you try your hardest, and you still can't do it, I'll ask the raccoons to stick to the traditional music for the rest of the dance. What do you think?"

Breeze thought for a moment. And then she grinned and nodded. "Yes," she said. "I can agree to that."

Cressida smiled at her unicorn friends. "Do we have a plan that's okay with all of you?"

"Yes!" Moon, Breeze, and Firefly all said at once.

"Well done!" said Cressida. "It usually takes my brother Corey and me a lot longer to reach a compromise. I'm impressed."

The unicorns grinned.

Moon looked at Cressida. “Magic Princess Cressida, I think we’re ready to build a brand new ballroom.”

Cressida smiled and gripped her magic wand.

Chapter Eight

Cressida walked to the edge of the circle of mud and rocks and waved her wand at the ground. The star-shaped sapphire at the end sparkled, and light poured out. Instantly, a thick, pink vine sprouted. This time, Cressida held the wand over the vine and lifted upward as far as she could, until the vine was nearly as tall as her mother. Then, still holding up the wand, Cressida took a step to her right. To her relief and delight, more vines instantly grew from the ground.

Cressida slowly walked around the edge of the muddy circle, growing a longer and longer circular wall of vines with each step. When she was only a few feet away from the place where she had begun, she made an arcing motion with her wand to form a doorway. Then Cressida stepped back and smiled at the pink, tangled vines that enclosed the new ballroom.

"Ta da!" Cressida said.

"I'm glad there's now at least a ballroom," Moon said, "but what about the floor? Do we have to dance in the mud?"

"I hope not," Cressida said, though she had to admit dancing in the mud might be at least a little bit fun. She looked at Breeze and asked, "Do you think you could send a giant gust of wind to bring all of Moon's Midnight Stars to the new ballroom?"

"Excellent idea!" Breeze said. The aquamarine on her ribbon necklace shimmered and blue glittery light shot out from her horn. Then a comet-shaped gust of wind appeared. It danced in circles above the wall of pink vines and then bolted away toward the thick part of the forest where the Midnight Stars lived. A few seconds later, a swirling cyclone of gray stars twisted toward them and entered the ballroom through the arched entrance. Inside, the wind turned into a blizzard that filled the air with stars. Then, with one final gust, they fluttered downward into a pile on the floor.

"I know what to do now!" Moon said, grinning. She pointed her horn toward the sky. Her opal shimmered as sparkling light poured from her horn. Suddenly,

everything went pitch black. After a few seconds, the stars began to glow again, brightening as they turned from white to yellow to orange to red.

"Midnight Stars, make a dance floor, please!" Moon called out.

The Midnight Stars lifted off the ground and swirled above the mud and rocks. Then, they dropped down to form a perfect red, glowing floor for the ballroom.

"Excellent work, Breeze and Moon," Cressida said.

When she turned to her unicorn friends she noticed that Breeze's gust of wind had left their tails and manes a frizzy, windblown mess. She reached up and touched her own hair. It felt like a bird's nest that was even more tangled than the vines that formed the ballroom's walls.

"I guess we're all going to have messy hair for the ball," Firefly said.

"We'll start a new fashion trend," Cressida said. "We can call it the Breezy Look!"

Breeze laughed. "It's special style that's just for dancing to the new music," she said, winking at Moon.

Cressida grinned. "Now I think we need just a little more light," she said, turning to Firefly. "Do you think you could create a swarm of fireflies that will hover above our new ballroom?"

"What a fantastic idea," Firefly said. She pointed her horn toward the ceiling. Her gemstone, an orange citrine, shimmered. Orange light shot from her horn. And then a cloud of fireflies appeared above the new ballroom so the inside glowed a warm yellowy red.

"I love it!" Moon said. "I think this new

ballroom is even better than the old one! Thank you, Magic Princess Cressida!"

"Yes, thank you," Breeze and Firefly said at once.

Chapter Nine

Cressida slid her magic wand into one of her pockets and paused to admire their hard work. Just then Sunbeam, Flash, Bloom, and Prism arrived for the ball. For a moment, they stared in surprise at the new ballroom, with its pink vine walls, red star-tiled floor, and firefly ceiling. And then they smiled.

"I absolutely love the new ballroom,"

Prism said. "But what happened to the old one?"

"And what happened to your manes and tails?" Bloom asked, giggling.

"And why are you absolutely covered in mud?" Flash asked.

"And Cressida," Sunbeam said, rearing up with delight, "where did you get that crown?"

Moon and Cressida told Flash, Sunbeam, Bloom, and Prism the story of the missing ballroom, the magic crown and wand, the compromise, and the new ballroom. "We've given Cressida a new name," Breeze said. "Now we call her Magic Princess Cressida."

"Anytime you need someone to make

pink vines grow, you know who to ask," Cressida said, giggling.

"And," Firefly added, "we're calling our messy hair the Breezy Look. It's a special style that's just for dancing to the new music."

"Well, in that case," Sunbeam said, smiling playfully, "don't you think we all need to have the Breezy Look?"

Flash, Bloom, and Prism looked uncertain.

"I just spent hours getting my mane and tail ready for the ball," Flash said. But then she shrugged, smiled, and said, "Oh, why not?"

Bloom and Prism nodded.

"Four more Breezy Looks coming right up!" Breeze said. The aquamarine on her necklace twinkled, blue glittery light poured from her horn, and then a little blue gust of wind appeared. It swirled in circles around Sunbeam, Flash, Bloom, and Prism until their manes and tails looked even messier than Moon's, Breeze's, and Firefly's.

"How do I look?" Bloom asked. Her green mane was so tangled Cressida could hardly see her emerald crown.

"Absolutely breezy," Cressida said.

"Is that mud part of the style for dancing to the new music too?" Bloom asked, looking at Cressida's ball gown and sneakers and Moon's hooves, legs, and cape.

"Not really," Moon said.

Cressida shook her head. She didn't really mind the mud. But she supposed that if she were about to go to a ball, it might be nice to have a clean ball gown.

"Allow me to help," Bloom said. Her emerald glittered. She pointed her horn at a large mud stain on Cressida's gown. Glittery light shot out, and the spot of mud shrank until Cressida couldn't see it. Bloom kept shrinking the splattered mud until Cressida's ball gown looked as clean as it had when Ernest first made it. Then she shrank all the splatters of mud on Moon.

"Thank you!" Cressida and Moon said at the same time.

Just then, Cressida turned around and spotted Ringo, Renee, Roland, and Rita walking toward them. The raccoons, wearing their tuxedos, carried harps, drums, flarpophones, quadruple-duple-banjinanos, trumpledumpledordions, and octogolocto-horns. "We love the new ballroom!" Ringo said as he and his friends walked through the entrance and began to set up their instruments.

"I'm so excited, I can't stand it!" Moon said. "And I'd better go tell the raccoons about our music compromise." She galloped into the ballroom and then leaped and spun across the floor toward the raccoons. Cressida and the other unicorns followed her into the ballroom. The stars sparkled like rubies as Cressida stepped on them, and she spun and twirled on the new dance floor. It was absolutely perfect for dancing.

Suddenly, Ernest skipped into the ballroom in his tuxedo, which now had tails instead of kale. And right behind him filed in more different creatures than Cressida could count, all wearing tuxedos and ball gowns. There were dragons, foxes, rabbits, gnomes, elves, mini-dragons, fairies, cats, butterflies, wolves, turtles, and birds. Cressida even noticed a red bird with messy feathers in the brightest, reddest ball gown she could imagine.

Cressida heard Ringo counting out loud, just the way he had in the hollow tree, and then the raccoons began to play the song they had played for Moon and Cressida. At first, all the unicorn princesses except Moon froze, unsure of how to dance.

Moon trotted up to her sisters and said, "Magic Princess Cressida taught me that this is a kind of music that you can dance to in any way you want. There are no rules or steps or right ways or wrong ways. Just close your eyes and movc in whatever way feels best."

Sunbeam and Prism grinned, closed their eyes, and immediately began to twirl, jump, and spin. Bloom and Flash watched for several seconds, shrugged, and shut their eyes. At first they just swayed to the beat, but soon they were doing what looked like a square dance. Breeze and Firefly stood stiffly, looking uncomfortable. Moon smiled reassuringly and said, "I think I felt exactly the same way you do now when I first tried to dance to this song. Just close your eyes and give it a try!"

"Do you promise not to laugh at us?" Breeze asked.

"Absolutely," Moon said. "I promise."

Breeze and Firefly closed their eyes. They shuffled back and forth for several seconds. And then they began to tap their hooves. "That's right," Cressida said encouragingly. She tapped her unicorn sneakers along with them.

Next, Breeze began to swish her tail and shake her head. And Firefly nodded with the beat and shuffled her front feet. "Excellent," Moon said.

And then, to Cressida's delight, Breeze and Firefly began to dance along with everyone else. Soon, Cressida, Flash, Sunbeam, Bloom, Prism, Breeze, and Firefly were leaping, kicking, spinning, swaying, shimmying, and twirling.

At the end of the song, Moon, breathless from dancing, exclaimed, "This is the best Starlight Ball we've ever had! Thank you, Magic Princess Cressida!"

"Yes," agreed Breeze and Firefly. "Thank you."

Before Cressida could respond, the raccoons launched into a traditional unicorn song. Again, all the unicorns began to dance. The song reminded Cressida of the music for her dance recital that weekend, and she used some of the steps she had been practicing at home that afternoon.

Cressida and the unicorns danced to song after song, until Ringo announced, "This will be our last song!"

Cressida felt disappointed—she could have danced for at least two more hours—but she was also hungry and thirsty. As the band started to play one of their new songs, the unicorns rushed over to Cressida and formed a circle around her.

"Thank you so much for saving the Starlight Ball," Flash said.

"We're going to name this the Magic Princess Cressida Ballroom in honor of you," Moon said.

"I'm so glad I could help," Cressida said.

As the raccoons played the final notes

of the last song, Cressida said, "Thank you for inviting me to your ball. I've had a wonderful time, but I think I'd better return to the human world now."

"See you soon!" Moon said.

"We had so much fun dancing with you!" Sunbeam said.

"We can't wait for your next visit!" Flash said.

Bloom, Prism, and Breeze said, "Good-bye, Magic Princess Cressida!"

And Firefly nodded and winked.

Cressida pulled her key from her pocket. She wrapped both hands around the crystal-ball handle and closed her eyes. "Take me home, please," she said.

Immediately, the ballroom began to spin

into a pink blur, and then everything went pitch black. Cressida felt as though she were lifting off from the ground and soaring through the sky. And then she landed on something wet. At first, all she could see was a swirl of gray, green, and brown. But soon the woods stopped spinning, and she found herself sitting on the soggy ground, right beneath the giant oak tree.

Next to her, the yellow-and-black-striped umbrella leaned against the tree trunk. She was wearing her rainbow leggings, her T-shirt with the star design, her green raccoon sweatshirt, and her silver unicorn sneakers. She touched her head, hoping her crown might still somehow be there. She felt her hair, tangled from Breeze's gust of wind and all her enthusiastic dancing. Though the crown was gone, she felt something small and metal in her hair. She pulled it out to discover a gold barrette dotted with pink sapphires. Cressida grinned and put it back in her hair. She picked up and opened the umbrella. And then she skipped home as her unicorn sneakers blinked.

Join Cressida on her next magical adventure!

Turn the page for a glimpse . . .

In the library at Pinewood Elementary School, Cressida Jenkins stood in front of the shelf with all the books about unicorns. There were twelve books total. She had read every single one at least twice. She had read five of them three times. And there were her two favorites—*An Illustrated Guide to Forest Unicorns* and *The Unicorn Encyclopedia*—that she had checked out and read cover-to-cover six times.

Cressida pulled *The Unicorn Encyclopedia* off the shelf. It had been a few weeks since she last read it, and she wanted to look at

her favorite picture: a giant, fold-out portrait of an orange, sparkling unicorn that reminded her of her friend, Princess Firefly. Cressida sat down on the library's blue carpet and flipped to page 17. She opened the flaps and smiled as she looked at the unicorn, who resembled Firefly in every way except that the unicorn in the book wasn't wearing a black ribbon necklace with a magic orange citrine gemstone.

Cressida loved the unicorn books in her school library, but she found herself wishing, right then, that there was a book all about the Rainbow Realm—a secret, magical world ruled by her friends, the unicorn princesses. How wonderful it would be, she thought, to open a book and see pictures of yellow Princess Sunbeam, silver Princess Flash, green Princess Bloom, purple Princess Prism, blue Princess Breeze, black Princess Moon, and orange Princess

Firefly. As she listed the unicorns' colors in her head, she paused. Why, she wondered, wasn't there a pink unicorn in the Rainbow Realm? And, for that matter, why wasn't there a unicorn that could fly?

That's when she had an idea that made her stand up and hop with excitement right there in the middle of the library. The second she got home from school, she would start writing and illustrating her very own book about the Rainbow Realm. And not only would she include the unicorns she already knew, but she would draw and write about a new pink flying unicorn too. Now she just needed to think of a name. Maybe Star or Sky or Wings or—

Ms. Wilcox, the school librarian, clapped

her hands three times. "It's time to check out your books and return to your classroom," she said.

Cressida closed *The Unicorn Encyclopedia* and stood up. As she walked through a maze of shelves toward the front desk, she kept imagining her book. Maybe the first page would be a giant picture of Spiral Palace, the unicorns' horn-shaped home. And after that—

"Cressida, are you ready to check out that book?" Ms. Wilcox asked.

Cressida had been so caught up in her plans that she hadn't even noticed she was standing right in front of Ms. Wilcox's desk.

"Yes, please," Cressida said, smiling

and handing Ms. Wilcox *The Unicorn Encyclopedia*.

"You had the biggest grin I think I've ever seen on anyone's face just now," Ms. Wilcox said. "What were you thinking about?"

Cressida never told adults—even kind adults like Ms. Wilcox—about the Rainbow Realm. Adults never seemed to understand that unicorns were real, and Cressida knew they would think she had simply imagined the unicorn princesses. "I was thinking about writing my own book," Cressida said.

"Well, that's a lovely idea," Ms. Wilcox said, and she stamped the page in the back of *The Unicorn Encyclopedia*.

"Thank you," Cressida said. And then she joined her friends Gillian and Eleanor as they lined up by the library door.

When Cressida got home from school, she dropped her pink unicorn backpack by the front door and dashed into the kitchen, where she grabbed a chocolate-chip granola bar and a glass of water. She walked down the hall to her bedroom as fast as she could without spilling her drink. She closed the door so her older brother, Corey, wouldn't disturb her. And then she pulled a drawing pad and a box of art supplies from her closet and set them out on her desktop.

She could already see the cover of her

UNICORN

book in her head. The title, *The Rainbow Realm*, would be in big letters across the front. And then, underneath, she would draw a picture of all the unicorn princesses, including the pink one she had just invented, standing together in front of Spiral Palace. Under the picture, in smaller letters, she would write, "by Cressida Jenkins."

The first thing Cressida wanted to do, even before she drew the cover, was to find a way to make a book from several blank pieces of paper. Maybe, she thought, she could try folding a stack of paper in half and then stapling it together along the crease. But just as she began to rummage around in her art supplies box for a stapler, she heard a high, tinkling noise.

Cressida froze, and her heart skipped a beat with excitement. The high, tinkling noise grew louder, and Cressida leaped over to her bedside table, opened the drawer, and pulled out an old-fashioned key with a crystal ball handle that hummed and glowed bright pink. The key had been a gift from the unicorn princesses so that Cressida could visit the Rainbow Realm any time she wanted: all she had to do was push the key into a tiny hole in the base of an oak tree in the woods behind her house. The unicorn princesses had also told her that when they wanted to invite her to the Rainbow Realm for a special occasion, they would make the key's handle glow bright pink—just the way it was glowing right then!

At that moment, the only thing that sounded more fun to Cressida than writing a book about the Rainbow Realm was visiting the Rainbow Realm. She pushed the key into the back pocket of her jeans. She looked down to make sure her shirt—an orange top with a yellow, glittery firefly design on the front—didn't have any large grape-juice or tomato-sauce stains from lunch. She had been in such a hurry to start her book project that she hadn't even taken off her shoes: silver unicorn sneakers with bright pink lights that blinked every time she walked, jumped, or ran. She finished her water in three giant gulps and ate her granola bar in two huge bites. And then she ran out of her room and down the hall to the living room, where her mother sat reading a book and drinking coffee.

"I'm going for a quick walk in the woods," Cressida said as she sprinted to the back door. Time in the human world froze while Cressida was in the Rainbow Realm, so even if Cressida stayed with the unicorn princesses for hours, her mother would think she had been gone only a few minutes.

"Have a great time," her mother said.

Cressida sprinted across her back yard and into the woods. With her sneakers blinking, she ran along the path that led to the magic oak tree. When she got there, she pulled the key from her back pocket, kneeled at the tree's base, and pushed the key into a tiny hole.

Suddenly, the woods began to spin into a blur of green leaves, blue sky, and brown tree trunks. Then everything went pitch black, and Cressida had the sensation of falling fast through space. After several seconds, Cressida landed on something soft, and all she could see was a dizzying swirl of silver, white, pink, and purple. Soon the spinning slowed to a stop, and Cressida knew exactly where she was: sitting on a gigantic pink velvet armchair in the front hall of Spiral Palace.

Emily Bliss lives just down the street from a forest. From her living room window, she can see a big oak tree with a magic keyhole. Like Cressida Jenkins, she knows that unicorns are real.

Sydney Hanson was raised in Minnesota alongside numerous pets and brothers. She has worked for several animation shops, including Nickelodeon and Disney Interactive. In her spare time she enjoys traveling and spending time outside with her adopted brother, a Labrador retriever named Cash. She lives in Los Angeles.

www.sydwiki.tumblr.com

LOOK FOR THESE OTHER MAGICAL CHAPTER BOOK SERIES!

Butterfly Wishes BY JENNIFER CASTLE

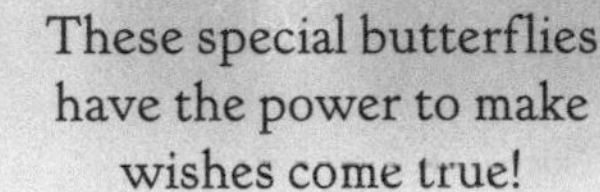

These special butterflies have the power to make wishes come true!

www.bloomsbury.com
Facebook: KidsBloomsbury
Twitter: BloomsburyKids

Magic Animal Rescue

BY E. D. BAKER

When magical creatures need help,
it's Maggie to the rescue!

www.bloomsbury.com
Facebook: KidsBloomsbury
Twitter: BloomsburyKids

Princess Ponies

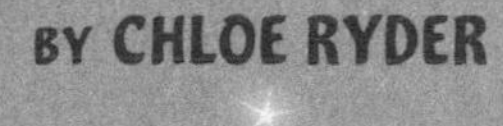

Don't miss Pippa's journey to find the golden horseshoes and save Chevalia!

www.bloomsbury.com
Facebook: KidsBloomsbury
Twitter: BloomsburyKids

Kitty's magic

by Ella Moonheart

Kitty is no ordinary girl. . . . She can transform into a cat!

• COMING SOON •

www.bloomsbury.com
Facebook: KidsBloomsbury
Twitter: BloomsburyKids